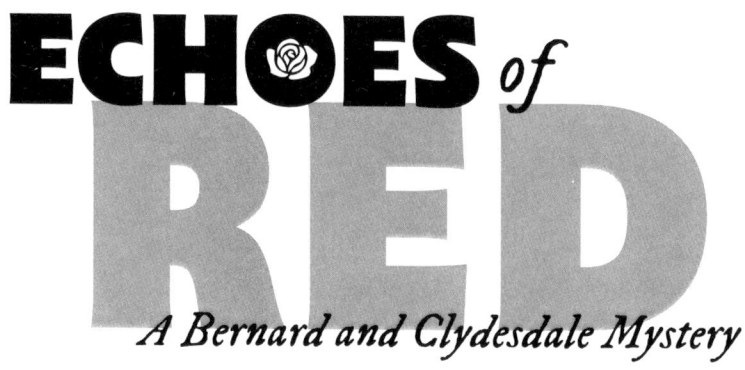

ECHOES of RED

A Bernard and Clydesdale Mystery

MARGARET CRAVENS

© Margaret Cravens

ISBN: 978-1-66787-572-9
eBook ISBN: 978-1-66787-573-6

All rights reserved. This book or any portion thereof may not be reproduced or used in any manner whatsoever without the express written permission of the publisher except for the use of brief quotations in a book review.

A massive thank you to my family, my friends, and the amazing Severn School librarians. You have been incredible ears, editors, and emotional supports.

PROLOGUE:

It was late in the little town of Closefield Springs, or early, depending on how you chose to look at it. Most people were sound asleep, and had been for hours. They were tucked up in their warm and comfortable beds, snoring loudly, as fluffy mid-January snow swirled down outside their windows. Most people were asleep, but not all.

Ben Clydesdale's wife was fast asleep, but though he lay right beside her in their bed, Ben was not. He was staring up at the ceiling, trying to shake the nervous trembly feeling that remained with him after a nightmare. His cat mewed softly in the darkness, and in his nervous state, he very nearly cried out in fear, but he stopped himself in time. He didn't want to wake Lila.

On the other side of town, in the small apartment she shared with her younger brother, Julie Bernard was also wide awake, tapping away on the keyboard of her old computer and trying desperately to finish an article for the Closefield Times that was due the very next day. Or, more accurately, later that same day. She paused to yawn and take a sip of coffee, flexed her fingers, which were beginning to tighten and cramp, and continued on. Her brother snored loudly in the other room, but there would be no sleep for her tonight.

Downtown, at Roscoe Restaurant and Bar, a large and slightly boisterous party was just beginning to wind down. Most of the guests left through the front doors, shaking hands as they left with the host, a tall woman with curly dark hair and rectangular glasses. Some, however, chose to trickle out the back door. They emerged in the parking lot and staggered past the dumpsters toward the street and home. They did not look up at the radio station, which shared its back parking lot with Roscoe, as they stumbled past, nor did they spare a thought for the other people awake behind those few lighted windows.

Behind one of those windows, and a set of crooked grayish blinds, Caleb Fredrick's bleeding body was dragged across the green-and-white carpet and stuffed unceremoniously behind the sofa, leaving behind a trail of blood and ash from his half-smoked cigarette.

The sun rose, and the sleeping people woke, got up, filled mugs with coffee, and started going about their day. For Alex Harcourt, this meant looking for her employer who had not returned home the night before. That was not particularly unusual for him; it had happened twice before that month. He would get so tired after his show was done, that sometimes he'd fall asleep in the break room afterward. Still, normally he'd have texted or called home by then, and so Caleb's wife had sent Alex to find him.

"Caleb? Are you in here?" Alex called, as she poked her head into the break room. The lights were off, and there was a dark stain on the floor, which curved around from the middle of the room, past the cheesy cat calendars that no one remembered putting up to behind the battered blue striped couch. Alex hoped whatever it was would wash out quickly, before Brittany, the station's manager, would see it, and she checked the furniture for a sleeping Caleb.

However, Caleb was not, as Alex had expected, sleeping on the faded and tattered couch that took up a good third of the room. Neither was he lying sprawled on the ragged leather armchair, or getting breakfast or a cup of coffee at the faux marble counter that served as a kitchenette. Alex walked over to the light switch, her designer sneakers making barely a sound against the green and white diamond pattern of the carpet. She flicked on the lights, and something that she had thought was a shadow now appeared to be a black tennis shoe, poking out from behind the couch. Then she saw the ragged cuff of a pair of black jeans. She gasped and ran to her fallen employer, and screamed.

It was a gruesome sight. Caleb was lying face-down on the carpet, which had been stained dark by a now-dry puddle of blood. A large kitchen knife stuck out from his back like a porcupine's quill.

The police swarmed down upon the radio station like moths drawn to a flame. The detective in charge of the case, a scrawny, ferret-like man by the name of Arnold McMillan, spent the entire afternoon barking orders at everyone within shouting distance, at a volume that made even his colleagues, who were used to his antics, wince.

Once it was established that the dead DJ's wallet was missing, and that the weapon used to stab him had been part of the knife set in the kitchenette of the radio station, McMillan concluded that the DJ's death had been the unfortunate result of a robbery. He still asked all the usual questions, but when no alternative theories presented themselves, he doubled down on his opinion of the killer as a "junky delinquent off the streets, just looking for some drug money," as he phrased it to one of his subordinates in a very self-satisfied tone of voice.

But soon a day, then a week, and then a month passed, and Caleb's wallet was still untraceable, and no alternative leads yielded results. Arnold stopped strutting around like he owned the town and began justifying his investigation in what bordered on a rant to anyone who dared pose even the smallest question or criticism. The townspeople stopped discussing the murder amongst themselves and started moving on with their lives, but by no means did they forget about it. These things have a way of being remembered.

CHAPTER 1:
The Girl in the Bar

In the good old days, Smoky's had been Ben's favorite place to go for a drink after a hard day's work, not for its quality, which was mediocre at best, but because it was convenient and cheap. He had lots of good memories there, making friends, letting off steam, laughing, smiling. That had been a long time ago, about ten years, and it felt like another lifetime. Now, as he stood under the sagging red awning and peered in through the green glass windows, Ben weighed the shelter from the icy winds against his reluctance to face those memories.

The cold wore him down. He swung open the thick wooden door. The heat that washed over him reduced his reluctance, but did not eliminate it in its entirety.

The room hadn't seemed to have changed a bit in the intervening years. The round red tables were still covered in unidentified sticky substances. The long rough wooden bar still tilted forward slightly, which probably still caused the occasional spilled drink. The carpet still had mysterious stains, including Old Man Smoky, a dark stain in one corner that looked sort of like a face, if you looked at it from the right angle with unfocused eyes. The bar stools were still covered in the same vinyl coverings, held together with duct tape and prayers. The lighting was still dim but friendly. The dart board in the corner looked perhaps a bit more ragged, but that was the only real change as far as Ben could see.

The girl currently attacking the dartboard was one of the youngest people there. Most of the patrons that day were sporting guns and badges, and approaching middle age. Ben had been among them, ten years ago, not those people exactly, but people like them. The girl by the dartboard, however, couldn't have been older than twenty-five, and Ben had never seen anyone so unlike a cop before in his life. She had an unkempt mass of caramel-colored hair and big hazel eyes which flashed with anger as her darts whipped through the air to land with solid thunks on the decrepit dart board.

At the sight of those angry hazel eyes, recognition flitted through Ben like an electrical current, but it was gone almost as soon as it had come. He ordered a drink, trying to ignore the hair standing up on the back of his neck. He thanked the bartender without really seeing him and took his drink over to a crumb-covered table near the girl. He eyed her through his battered wire-rimmed glasses as he raised the beer to his lips.

The girl glanced over her shoulder. Ben tried to look away, but he was too slow. Their eyes met. The girl set her darts down on the table closest to her and walked over to him.

"You've come back, then," she said in a stiff voice.

"Do I know you?" Ben asked. His heart seemed to be beating much faster than usual. He knew this girl, he was sure of it, but he couldn't place her.

The girl snorted. "Yeah, been a while. I was what, fifteen, last time I saw you?"

Ben felt like his heart had dropped to his stomach. "Julie Bernard," he said.

Julie's lips twitched in a joyless smile. "That's me."

"After all this time," Ben muttered.

"What're you doing here? I didn't expect to see you anywhere near my Dad."

"Is he here now?" Ben asked, looking around in alarm.

Julie laughed and pulled out a seat at Ben's table with a squeaking clatter. "Nah. He's probably at home and asleep by now."

"So…." Ben said, trying desperately to think of something to say. "How've you been?"

"Quit my job today," Julie said, with the first note of true cheerfulness she'd shown the entire interaction. "I was working as a reporter for the Closefield Times. I wanted to look into Caleb Fredrick's death. They said no. I walked out."

"I'm sorry," Ben said.

"Eh. My family will be disappointed. They all thought I'd finally found my calling as a reporter. Well, I haven't, and that's the truth, and if that makes them upset, then so be it," Julie said, kicking her feet up onto the table and leaning back in the shabby wooden chair.

"Why do you want to know about Caleb Fredrick?" Ben asked, more to change the subject than anything else.

"It's a murder, isn't it? I mean, I only got into reporting in the first place because Dad wouldn't let me do detective stuff. And then a murder happens right under our noses, and they expect me to write about the mayor's dog," Julie said. Her eyes had taken on a sort of hungry look. Ben recognized it immediately. He'd seen it before, not on Julie, but on her father, whenever he'd been working a particularly complex or thrilling case.

"You don't think it was a robbery, then?" Ben asked.

"Of course, I don't think it was a robbery!" Julie said. "And I don't see why the police do, either. There was a ton of valuable equipment in the place. Any proper thief would have taken something else beside a wallet."

"That's what I thought," Ben said. Julie nodded. Then the full implications of the statement hit her, and she looked up.

"You mean you're looking into it too?" Julie asked, her eyes wide. Ben fished through his massive pockets, drawing out a chewed-up cat toy, a pack of gum, and a small flashlight before finally producing a stack of business cards and handing one to Julie.

Julie studied the card. "Private detective?" she asked, a grin slowly spreading over her face.

"It's not as interesting as it sounds. Mostly people wanting dirt on their spouses so that they can get better divorce settlements."

"But you have a murder," Julie said, and she took her feet off the table so that she could lean forward. "Who hired you?"

"Sydney Fredrick. Caleb's wife," Ben said. Julie nodded.

The bell over the door rang. Ben looked up to see Lila entering. She spotted them and walked over to the table.

"Are you ready to go?" she asked Ben.

"Yeah, in a minute. Just got to pay," Ben said, gathering up his things.

"I've got it. You go," Julie said.

"Right." Ben would have been lying if he'd said that it'd been nice, catching up with Julie. It had been awkward, and painful as well. She wasn't the neon-clad kid he remembered.

"I... I have notes, you know, on Caleb Fredrick. I…" Julie blushed. "I was looking into his death, a little. On my own, you know, kind of like a hobby. Do you want to see them?" Julie asked, fidgeting with the sleeve of her baggy black coat.

"Oh! Well, yeah, that'd be great. Two sets of eyes is always better than one."

"When do you want them?" Julie asked. There was a hint of contained excitement in her voice, a slightly breathless quality, as if the words were simply rushing out too fast for her oxygen intake to keep up.

"Does tomorrow work? Just bring them by the office. Address on the card."

"Tomorrow, then," Julie said, and then Ben followed Lila into the wintery night.

"Was that Julie Bernard?" Lila asked as they got into the car.

"Yup," Ben said, not quite believing it himself.

Julie sat frozen in her seat after Ben left, her mind whirling. There was just so very much going on. She'd always wanted to solve a murder, ever since she was young. Well, younger. The idea had always appealed to her. It had first started when she'd begun to understand what her father did for a living, and soon she'd become determined to be just like him, saving lives and bringing justice to an unjust world, or something like that. In high school, even after the Incident, murder mysteries had been her retreat from reality, a safe place for her to hide. The detectives in the shows had Incidents like hers, but they just kept going on with their lives, and in a season or two, you could forget that anything had ever happened. When she'd tried to explain that to her family she'd gotten some very worried looks, so she'd dropped the subject. So in college, when she'd started looking at careers properly, she'd figured being a reporter would be close enough, as close as she was going to get, the way things were, but now… Now she had a chance to do what she'd always dreamed of.

But also whirling around the tornado that was her thoughts, chasing the excitement away and leaving behind a cold knot in her stomach, were the memories of the Incident. It hadn't been Ben's fault, but just seeing him had been enough to drag up those memories from the places inside herself where she'd buried them away and thrust them into the front of her mind. She didn't think about the Incident much anymore, it had been so long ago, but she thought about it now.

A growling stomach saved Julie from a possibly perpetual cycle of painful self-reflection. She ordered nachos and leaned back in her chair. When she had eaten her fill, she wiped her greasy fingers on her already stained leggings and threw another dart at the board. It hit dead center, of course it did, after all, that's where she'd been aiming. Julie grinned to herself, paid the tabs, and left to brave the winter night.

She walked home quickly, with her head bowed, trying to hide from the cold and sleet within the folds of her big black woolen coat, but it got in anyway. Ice found its way down her collar and melted there against her skin, dripping down her back until she was soaked through and shivering. She saw the lights of her apartment building up ahead, and she quickened her pace to a trot. Finally, she ducked into the building and began trudging up the back stairs. Her footsteps made a hollow echoing noise as she climbed. She got to her landing, caught her breath, and threw open the door to the brightly-lit rooms she shared with her brother.

"You're late," Trip called, as she hung her coat on the rack. He was sitting at his drawing table with a sketchbook and charcoal, an island of serenity and organization in the cluttered and chaotic room. Trip was a slim young man, only a year out of college, with short neat-cut sandy blond hair and a pointed chin. He was tall, taller than their father even, and though he was dressed in sweatpants and a t-shirt, he still, as always, managed to look put-together and presentable.

"I guess," Julie said with a shrug, as she unlaced her grimy boots and tucked them next to Trip's pristine sneakers.

Trip wasn't finished. "What, were you on a date or something?" he asked, turning to look at her.

Julie snorted. "Or something."

Trip set down his sketchbook on top of the nearest pile of dog-eared and battered books. Piles like it were sprouting up all over the room, on the couch, the coffee table, the counter, the dinner table, even the floor. Adding more shelf-space had been on Julie's to-do list for years, and the piles of books were among the several complaints Trip made regularly about life in the apartment. But he didn't have to pay any rent, so he couldn't really complain.

At the moment, he had the same look in his eye as he did when he made those complaints, one of disappointment and exasperation. "Katie called. She said you quit."

Julie was taken aback for a moment. She hadn't told Katie that information yet. But Katie had a vast network of friends who were just as inquisitive and big-mouthed as she was. Julie sighed. She'd wanted to keep it a secret, for a few days at least, until she actually came up with a plan to get a new job, but it didn't look like that was going to be an option. "I guess so."

"Then it's true?!" Trip asked, jumping up from his stool.

"Yup," Julie said. Trip looked like he wanted to say something, probably along the lines of "what the hell were you thinking," but after a few minutes of painful jaw-grinding, he slowly sank back down into his chair.

"I could see if Annie knows of any openings—"

"No, Trip," Julie said, cutting him off. "I'll figure it out for myself. I'm going to bed."

Julie left Trip behind and shut the door to her bedroom, which was, if possible, even more cluttered than the living room and kitchen. Here the drifts of books had grown over almost every available surface and rose up to truly precarious heights. Julie sighed and rubbed her temples. Trip meant well, but often it felt like she had moved out of her parents' house only to move back in. Julie told herself she was being unfair and opened the desk drawer, pulling out the folder she'd dedicated to Caleb Fredrick. She'd covered it with rainbow stickers.

"Childish," Julie muttered, scraping them off with her fingernails so that Ben wouldn't see. She flipped through the folder and made some last-minute notes before setting it on top of her dresser, changing into pajama pants and a t-shirt, brushing her teeth, and turning out the light. 'All in all,' she thought, as she drifted off to sleep, 'it had been a good day.'

CHAPTER 2:
Old Friends

Ben had another nightmare that night. He'd used to have it regularly, but it had been almost five years since the last time. The dream had changed, in the time in-between. This time, Julie, the older Julie he'd met that evening, not the teenaged Julie from all those years ago, was standing at his shoulder, watching alongside him as her younger form bled on the carpeted floor. Darkness pressed close around them, all Ben could see was Julie (both of them) and the tiny patch of crusty carpet underfoot.

"It's your fault I am what I am. It's your fault I'm not who I'm supposed to be," Dream Julie had said.

"No! I didn't mean for this to happen! It was an accident!"

Dream Julie had looked down, at the younger version of herself lying at her feet, and then suddenly, the Julie by his shoulder had vanished, no, now it was she who lay bleeding on the floor. Then she faded away, like a dying Jedi, and Ben was alone, and the darkness was closing in.

"I'm sorry!" Ben shouted, but it was too late. She was gone. All around him there was nothing but solid darkness, and Julie's words echoing in the void: "It's your fault."

Ben woke up in a cold sweat. He looked around, panicking for a second, before he realized where he was. Light from the streetlights came in through the thin curtains, just enough for Ben to make out the shadows of the bedroom furniture. Next to him, Lila rolled over in her sleep. Her long silky hair had fallen across her dark elfish face. Gently, Ben tucked it behind her ear. He wished he could feel as calm and at peace as she looked, lying there. He checked his watch. He still had another three hours before he would get up for the day. Ben turned on his side and watched Ramona, their grumpy calico cat, as she slept in the window-seat; the fuzzy silhouette of her chest rose and fell softly.

When Lila's alarm went off at 5:45, Ben pretended to wake up with her. He showered, shaved, and dressed in one of his usual dark three-piece suits, before pouring himself a very large cup of coffee, which he hoped would serve as a satisfactory replacement for a full-night's sleep, though, he knew better.

Thirty minutes later, he was in his office downtown, pacing back and forth, his newest pair of dress shoes making hard clicks against the worn wooden floorboards, almost as if he were tap dancing. He had a lot of work to get done, but he couldn't focus on any of it. Looming over his mind was Julie's potential visit. He tried to work on any of his other cases, but after the seventh time he found himself staring off into space, he gave up.

Ben's office was located on the edge of what people termed "downtown," sandwiched between a personal injury law practice and a comic-book store. It was a narrow stone building, set slightly back from the street. A short flight of gray stone steps led up to the green door with the fogged glass window. "Benjamin K. Clydesdale: Private Investigator" was printed on the window in clean and fresh black and gold lettering.

The church bells were ringing noon as Julie Bernard climbed the stone steps and knocked twice on the green-painted door. Ben opened the door almost immediately. Julie was still wrapped in the same big black wool coat she'd had the night before, but underneath it she was wearing a pair of paint-splattered jeans and a green turtleneck sweater that was starting to unravel at the cuffs.

"Hello. Good morning. Well, noon, I suppose," Ben said.

"Good noon to you too," Julie said with a grin.

Ben suddenly realized that they were still standing on the steps. "I'll show you around."

He moved to the side and Julie stepped into the outer office.

It was a small room, almost completely filled by the large desk in one corner and the gray-green sofa against the wall. In the spaces not filled with furniture, Julie could see that the worn wooden floorboards were covered with an old rug, which had been purchased for Ben's first apartment over twenty-five years ago and by now was completely threadbare. On the wall opposite the sofa was the door to the inner office, which Ben opened next.

As soon as Ben swung the door to the inner office open, Julie was in love. The room could have been considered either cramped or cozy, depending on your personal preference. Julie was inclined toward cozy. There was a small window in one wall, and some light was able to come in from the streets through the thin green curtains, but even between that and the light fixtures, the room was on the dim side. A large desk was set opposite the window, made of elegant dark wood. The green-glass desk lamp perched on top of it cast a warm circle of light. Next to the window was a fraying armchair, covered in fabric that had once been yellow with orange striping, but it had been sun-faded and spilled on so much over the years that by now the original pattern was near invisible. The only piece of the room that looked like it was in the proper century was the row of three neat metal filing cabinets lined up on the far wall.

"Looks like something out of an old detective novel," Julie said at last.

"Is that a good thing?" Ben asked.

"Yeah."

They stood there awkwardly for a moment more, before Ben remembered the purpose of this meeting.

"Do you have the notes?"

Julie nodded and pulled a yellow plastic folder out of her worn messenger bag.

"That's everything. And I wrote down Luke Sebastian's number on the front, that's Caleb's best friend. Luke's a musician. My brother had his number from some event or another. All the local artists move in the same circles in a town like this," Julie said, sliding the folder across the desk. Ben opened it. Julie's handwriting was only just barely legible. Some portions seemed to have been written in a hurry, and the ones that weren't had been crammed into the margins of documents and photographs. But when he squinted and deciphered her writing, he could see that it was incredibly in-depth. She'd researched things he hadn't even thought to look into and answered questions he'd only just begun to ask.

"Your brother's a musician?"

"Yeah, but he's not very good."

"Did he know Caleb?"

"No. I asked when Caleb was killed. The best Trip could do was Luke."

"This is still pretty good."

Yet another awkward silence. This time it was Julie who broke it.

"Uh, well, I'll be going now. Promised Katie I'd meet her for lunch."

"Thanks for coming over. This is really helpful," Ben said.

Julie nodded and opened the door to leave, but paused with it ajar and turned back. "Wait, do you want my number? In case you have any questions about what I wrote?"

"Sure," Ben said, without really thinking about it. Julie scribbled her number down on a scrap of paper and handed it to him. Then she skipped out the door.

Ben watched from the little office window as Julie stepped outside. On the steps, when she thought no one was watching, she did a little victory dance. Ben grinned in spite of himself and turned back to the folder and his own notes. He had a murder to solve.

After her impromptu dance party, Julie walked down the block to the little café where she was supposed to meet her friend. The skies were clear and the sun was shining, but the wind bit at her as she walked. She was glad to push open the glass doors of the café and feel the heated air rush over her.

It was a small establishment on a street corner. Pedestrians in heavy coats bustled by, pausing to wait for the cars to pass before crossing the streets. Inside, the café was warm and cheerful. It was a bit late for breakfast and just before the lunch rush, so it was relatively empty.

"Jules!" Katie called, waving at Julie from a corner table. Julie walked over and sat down across from her friend.

Katie was a tall, red-haired dental student with an impeccable sense of fashion and frequent new boyfriends. She could be a horrid gossip and a drama queen, but Julie supposed, she herself wasn't the model friend either. Today, Katie was dressed in an earth-toned sweater-dress and thick black leggings under a massive pink coat, all accented, of course, with a pink scarf and a black hat and a nice faux-leather purse.

Katie began to talk before Julie even had a chance to sit down. "Is it true that you quit your job? I heard it from Matti, who heard it from her sister, Miranda, you know her, you met her at the Christmas party. Anyway, Miranda heard it from her friend Sam, who has a cousin who works at the Closefield Times. Jamie Randell, I think the name is? I tried to call you as soon as Matti told me, but you'd left your phone at home and it was Trip who picked it up, and he couldn't confirm it either way."

Katie said all of this very quickly and without pausing to draw breath.

"Is that why you asked me to lunch, then?" Julie asked, glancing at Katie over the top of her menu.

Katie grinned sheepishly and waited for Julie's answer.

Julie sighed. "Yes, I quit. I was tired of being kept off the real stories."

"This isn't about that business with the dead DJ, is it?" Katie asked. When Julie didn't meet her eyes, Katie gave an exasperated sigh. "Honestly, Jules! It was just a robbery. The reason they haven't caught the guy is because he probably skipped town or else is lying dead in a ditch somewhere."

"You don't get it, Katie," Julie started to say, but she trailed off. She'd had this argument with Katie twice before, and she knew from experience that all of the protests and arguments in the world would do nothing to ease the expression of deep concern on Katie's face. If she kept pressing, she'd only prolong the lecture.

"You're not a cop; you never were. The sooner you accept that, the sooner you'll be happy," Katie said. Julie forced a smile and took a sip from her glass of water.

"Look, I know what'll cheer you up. Dennis has a friend at work, Todd, I think the name is. He's totally your type. What if all four of us went out sometime?"

"No, Katie."

"Are you sure? He's quite good-looking. Tall, you know. Nice hair. Just give him a shot."

"I said no!" Julie said. It wasn't quite a shout, but it was still enough that the entire café went silent for a moment. Julie was very conscious of the eyes of strangers on her and her friend. Then the moment passed, and the normal background chatter resumed.

"Sorry," Julie muttered. "It's just… I dunno."

"When was the last time you went on a date, Julie?" Katie asked. "Or even hung out with a friend?"

"I have friends—" Julie started to say, but Katie interrupted her.

"Besides me or your brother."

"I met an old friend at a bar yesterday," Julie said. It wasn't exactly a lie, save that Ben wasn't exactly a friend, maybe an acquaintance at best, and 'met' implied that the interaction had been prearranged. But there had been a bar. That part was true, at least.

"Who?"

"You've never met him. He moved away when I was in high school."

Katie seemed dubious, but she didn't call Julie out for lying, which was somewhat of a relief.

For the rest of the meal, Katie at least pretended to have moved on. She didn't bring up Todd or Julie's career plans. She chattered on about Matti, and her classes, and the latest in the fashion world, and Julie nodded and made all the appropriate noises. When they'd finished eating, Katie insisted on paying the bill. Julie chose to read this as an expression of friendship and not of pity. Then Julie walked Katie back to her apartment.

It was then that Julie realized that she had absolutely nothing else to do for the rest of the day, so she went back home, watched television, and flicked through various horrible mobile games on her phone. She was very glad Trip was out at a friend's art show all afternoon and wasn't there to see her.

CHAPTER 3:
Better Shared

Sydney Fredrick was a small woman with spiky brown hair and big dark eyes. She didn't look very well, but Ben supposed that was to be expected. There were shadows under her eyes and her fluffy pink sweater hung over her shoulders as if it were on a clothes rack and not a human being. She sat perched on the edge of Ben's armchair and nervously fingered the small silver cross hanging from a fine chain around her neck as she spoke.

"Thank you again for helping us," she was saying. "It's just, the police said they were sure they'd catch him soon, but it's been almost a month Well, I figured the more people looking into it, the better."

"It's my job, ma'am," Ben said.

"I expect you don't work many cases like this. I'm sorry if I'm causing your agency any trouble."

"It's been a while, yes, but it's no trouble. It's good to be doing something real, instead of just splitting up marriages."

Sydney nodded. "Have you made much progress yet?"

"I've learned what I can about the police investigation. They focused a little heavily on the possibility of robbery. Right now I'm trying to track down and speak with the people who surrounded Caleb in the weeks leading up to his death. Then we put together the story."

"Didn't the police do that?" Sydney asked, her brow furrowed.

"In theory, but most of their questions ended up coming back to the robbery. They weren't really looking for other possibilities."

Sydney nodded and thanked Ben again, and then she left. Ben, however, remained at his desk long afterward, looking through files, looking for any possible connection, even after the streetlights turned on and evening faded to night. He sighed, picked up the phone, and dialed the number for the radio station.

"Hello?" a receptionist said.

"Hello, I'm Ben Clydesdale, I'm a private investigator. I want to talk about Caleb Fredrick. I was wondering if I could speak to the manager."

Ben heard indistinct whispering on the other end of the line as the receptionist conferred with someone else.

"She's not in at the moment," the receptionist said at last. "You can always try her home number, though. I'll give it to you."

"Thank you," Ben said, and he grabbed a notepad and a pen. He wrote down the number the receptionist gave him, and then he hung up.

He tried the home number immediately afterward, but there was no response. Ben left a message, but he wasn't particularly hopeful.

The last number he called was the one Julie had given him for Luke Sebastian.

"Hey there," a voice drawled on the other end of the phone.

"Is this Luke Sebastian?" Ben asked.

"This is he. Who're you?"

"I'm Ben Clydesdale, I'm a private detective looking into the death of Caleb Fredrick. I understand you were friends? I wondered if we could talk."

There was a short pause before Luke replied. "Yeah, we were friends. What do you want to know?"

"Could we meet somewhere to talk? When are you free?"

"I guess I'm free tomorrow. You cool with meeting over lunch? There's this restaurant, um, the Palatine. I can meet you there at noon, yeah? That work?"

"That's fine," Ben said, and he thanked Luke and hung up.

It was nearing 10:00 now, and Ben was still sitting at his desk; Caleb's file still open in front of him. It was filled with names that meant nothing, events he didn't know the purpose of, and music jargon that might as well have been ancient Greek for all the meaning he could get out of it.

Julie would understand it. The dingy scrap of paper with her number on it sat temptingly in the golden light of the green desk lamp. It would be so easy to make one more call, ask her to come in again, help him with this whole thing.

He remembered his dream from the night before and shuddered; the scrap of paper lost some of its temptation. Still, the idea lingered, a little voice in the back of his head that refused to be silenced.

Ben heard the office door open but it didn't register in his mind until Lila rested her hand on his shoulder.

"Come on," she said quietly. "It's late."

Ben craned his neck to try to read the watch on her wrist, but failed. "What time is it?"

"9:54," Lila said. She had only just changed out of her work clothes. She wore gray sweatpants under her designer coat, and Ben could still see the kinks in her long dark hair; the result of having spent the day tied up in a braided bun. He caught a whiff of her peppermint shampoo as she handed him his coat from the rack.

"Hypothetically," Ben said, as he stood up. "What if I knew someone who could help me with this case? Who knew the world Caleb lived in and could help me navigate it? And who also happened to be a fair investigator in her own right?"

Lila held the door open for him as they walked out into the icy night. "Then I would tell you to call this person."

"But what if I was worried about this hypothetical person getting hurt? Because they may, hypothetically, have gotten hurt before? And because her hypothetical father might, hypothetically, come after and kill me if this person got hurt again?"

Lila sighed as they climbed into the battered old Honda CR-V. "I may have a guess as to who this hypothetical person is."

"Well?" Ben asked. "Should I ask her to help?"

"What does she want?" Lila asked.

"I think she would want to help. Probably too much. I worry she'll be too reckless. And I don't want her to get caught up in all of this again."

Lila shrugged. "If she wants to help, and you need her help, then I don't really see what the problem is. She's an adult now, she's capable of making her own decisions."

They pulled into the driveway and climbed up the narrow brick steps to the front door of their small two-bedroom home. It was a cheerful little house, painted yellow with a cherry red door and matching shutters. The doorknob stuck, like it always did.

The house was small but well-maintained. The furniture was simple but kept polished and neat, except for the scratches Ramona had inflicted upon the leather couch. The kitchen fixtures were shiny and the counter was clean. Neither of them had the energy to cook that night, so Lila ordered from the twenty-four-hour Italian place down the road, which had become a staple of their dinner rotations, and they sat down to eat and watch The Chronicles of Myst. The books were a favorite of theirs, but the movie adaptations that had come out while they were in college had disappointed. A few years ago, a TV show had been released, but they had been too busy at the time to watch it when it came out. They'd finally started watching it a few weeks ago, and it wasn't half-bad.

"Look," Lila said, when a car commercial broke in just as Rein Hallemar and Princess Cynthia (actually half-siblings, but if they were loyal to the books then that wouldn't be revealed for another few seasons) were fleeing through the woods as their home burned behind them. "You may have a responsibility to Julie, but you also have a responsibility to Caleb. Julie can choose to help you, she can choose to be reckless if it comes to it, but Caleb didn't choose to die. So doesn't your duty to him come first?"

Ben thought about that while Rein and Cynthia were defeating the evil lord Melodia's dragon-born minion. By that point in time, both Ben and Lila were falling asleep, so they paused the episode and went to bed.

Lila's alarm went off at 5:45 again, but this time she smashed the snooze button two or three times before finally dragging herself out of bed. Ben was glad. It was so much harder to justify staying in the nice warm bed if she was being a responsible adult.

"Have you decided what you're going to do about your hypothetical situation?" Lila asked, as she poured a large cup of coffee into a chipped green mug and handed it to him before fixing another for herself.

Ben studied his mug instead of responding.

Lila shrugged. "I've given you my take on the matter."

Ben sighed. "I think I'm going to call her. You're right, she's an adult, she can make her own decisions."

So, the first thing Ben did when he got to his office was dial the number Julie had scribbled onto the scrap of paper.

The blaring of her "nature" ringtone jerked Julie out of a relatively pleasant dream. She fumbled around her bedside table until she made contact with the device and picked up the call, if only to end the sound, which to her had always seemed more reminiscent of laser guns than birds chirping.

"Hello?" she asked, her voice muddy with sleep.

"Julie? It's Ben. Look, I'm realizing that I have a very limited understanding of Caleb's world, the music scene, that is, and you've already proven yourself capable. So, I was wondering if you would be interested in working for my agency? Just temporarily, while I'm working this case. I can pay you, I mean it won't be much, and it won't be official, but I can pay you. What do you say?"

It took a second for Ben's words to register, but once they had Julie was wide awake.

"How soon can I start?" she asked sounding almost girlish in her excitement.

"Can you come over today?"

"I'll be there in two hours."

CHAPTER 4:
A New Day

Julie knocked on the office door and held her breath. She felt very proud of herself for finding clean and un-tattered clothing to wear that morning, and not only brushing her hair, but putting on a headband as well, to keep loose strands clear of her face. This was the job of her dreams, after all. For once in her life, she wanted to make a good impression. All in all, she looked and felt presentable, which was better than she'd looked or felt in ages.

The door opened.

"You're early," Ben said, as he let her in.

"Better early than late. That's what Dad always says, anyway," Julie said. Ben nodded and showed her into the inner office. Julie set her leather messenger bag down on the fraying armchair and examined the whiteboard Ben had spent all morning setting up. In the center was a small picture of Caleb. Julie studied his face for a moment. He was on the attractive side, in a mildly feminine sort of way, and his dark brown hair was getting long, might even have been considered shaggy, had it not framed his face so well.

"What do we have so far?" Julie asked, pivoting on the balls of her feet to face Ben.

"Not much; not as much as I'd like, anyway," Ben said. "Killed by an ordinary kitchen knife, the big kind, you know, which was taken from the break-room, it had a kitchenette sort of thing. Stabbed in the back, went through the heart. No witnesses. No security cameras. No wallet."

"Do we know what was in the wallet, at least?"

"Nothing unusual, nothing that really stands out. Driver's license, credit cards, about fifty bucks in cash, a couple of coupons. But that's all according to Sydney, so it may have changed between when she last saw him that evening and when he was killed."

"What about the timeline?"

"His show finished at midnight. He stayed afterward to smoke a cigarette in the break room, which apparently he did every night. Sydney expected him home at one or two, but, obviously, he didn't show. It's all written up there," Ben said, pointing to the corresponding points on the whiteboard, each labeled in his neat spidery handwriting.

"And then time of death…"

"Around 1:00. I already asked around. Hardly anyone was in the building, just the DJ after Caleb, some guy called Duke Werkle."

"And the killer," Julie said, as she failed to raise an eyebrow.

"And the killer."

"Did the killer work at the radio station, do you think?" Julie asked.

"It's possible. Except that they all have alibis. Maybe we can poke holes in those alibis, maybe not."

Julie flopped down into the armchair, which creaked loudly in protest. "And you got all this from the police?"

"Yeah. You know, it's not that they didn't do their job. But they went down the wrong track, and now they're in a rut."

"Dad would never have done that," Julie muttered angrily.

"Your father wasn't on this case."

"Have you seen him, then? Since you got back?"

"To be honest, I've been trying to avoid him. Haven't spoken to him since, well, you know. I'm not proud; I know it's cowardly, but that's the truth."

"Maybe he's gotten over it. It's been ten years, after all."

Ben snorted. Then a thought occurred to him. "Why don't you blame me, Julie?" he asked, meeting her deep hazel eyes. Julie broke her gaze first, looking down at her hands instead of at him.

"I don't blame anyone, really, not even the guy who pulled the trigger, and I certainly don't blame you. It was bad, what happened, but…" she trailed off. For a moment Ben thought she might be trembling, but when she looked up and met his eyes, her gaze was steely.

"We have work to do."

"You're right," Ben agreed, relieved that she had changed the subject, and very much regretting bringing it up in the first place.

"What do we do first?"

"We're meeting Luke Sebastian for lunch today. I want to hear everything he knows about Caleb and the days leading up to his death."

"You think he knows something?" Julie asked, leaning forward. Even in the dim light, Ben could see that the hungry gleam was back in her eyes again.

"It's a start."

And so, at 11:55, Julie found herself walking through the double glass doors of the Palatine. It was a large restaurant, with lots of windows facing out onto the street. It had a laid-back atmosphere; the music was quiet, the patrons were happy, and the whole place smelled like good hot food. Julie surveyed the crowd of diners until she saw Luke. He was sitting next to a man Julie didn't recognize.

"There, that's him," Julie said, pointing to Luke for Ben's benefit. "The dark-haired one. I don't know who his friend is, though," and she led Ben over to the table and slid into the booth. Outside the large window, it was snowing again, cars rolled by with exaggerated care and people hurried along with their heads bowed and their hoods pulled up.

Luke looked Julie up and down. "Who're you?" he asked.

"I'm Julie Bernard. I think you've met my brother, Trip?"

"Oh, yeah, the guitarist. Nice dude. Well, I'm Luke, this is Cameron. I brought him along 'cuz he was friends with Caleb too."

Cameron nodded. He was about a head shorter than Luke, and stocky in build, with curly blond hair, dark brown eyes, and freckles. Both men were dressed in jeans and sweatshirts.

"You're Ben Clydesdale, then?" Luke asked, looking at Ben.

"Yes. So you were both close with Caleb?" Ben asked, pulling out his notepad and a pen.

"Yeah, since, like, forever," Luke said, reaching for his drink.

"When did you last see him?"

"We, all three of us, I mean, had lunch together the Sunday before he died. I know it was Sunday because he came in his church clothes," Luke said.

"I left early, though," Cameron added. "I had to meet my girlfriend. We were looking at apartments together."

"And that was your last contact with him?" Julie asked.

"Face to face, yeah. But the day before he died, he rang me up. Told me to meet him and Cam here… Christ, we were supposed to meet him the morning after he died. He said he had something to show me, or ask me, something like that, but anyway he didn't give me many details. Whatever it was, though, he made it sound serious."

"You have no idea what he wanted to discuss?" Julie asked.

"Not a clue. He'd never mentioned anything like it before, but…" Luke leaned forward, and his voice grew hushed. "If I had to guess, I'd say it was something to do with that flash drive he always had on him."

Ben looked up from his notepad. "What flash drive?"

"It was always with him. He treated it like the damn ring of power. Never told us what was on it, and got all cagey whenever we asked," Cameron said, without looking up from his chicken and potatoes.

Ben glanced at Julie out of the corner of his eye, but he kept most of his attention focused on the two young men. "Was it on him when he died?" he asked.

Cameron shrugged. "He kept with his wallet, I think, and that got stolen, right?"

"And you have no idea what was on it?"

"Not a clue. No one knows. I don't think even Sydney knows, and they told each other everything," Cameron said.

But Luke shook his head. "Alex might know. Alex Harcourt. She was Cal's assistant. If she doesn't know, she'll at least have a guess."

"One last thing. Where were you two the night Caleb was killed?" Ben asked.

Luke looked a little disgruntled at the question. "Like I told the cops, I was at home. My boyfriend was over, we were doing a game night sort of thing. His name's Leo Gardener, if that matters."

"Cameron?" Ben asked.

"Party. My girlfriend, Clarissa, she works at the radio station, and they'd just aired the 1000th episode of her show. We were all at the bar next door celebrating, her and me and most of her friends and a lot of the radio staff."

"Thank you both. You've been very helpful," Ben said, grabbing his coat and standing up. Julie followed his lead.

"I thought we knew their alibis already? From the police?" Julie asked as they braced to leave the warm shelter of the restaurant for the windy cold of the street.

"We did. I just wanted to confirm it. They're sticking to the same stories they told a month ago."

"What do we do now?"

"We talk to Alex Harcourt," Ben said with a grin.

CHAPTER 5:
Places to Be

Alex Harcourt was on vacation. Apparently, the shock of finding her employer brutally murdered had been a little traumatizing. She was in Wyoming with her brother and his family and would remain there for the rest of the month.

"So? What now?" Julie asked when Ben had gotten off the phone with Alex's parents and relayed this information to Julie.

"Someone has to know what was on that flash drive, or have an idea at least," Ben said. "I don't particularly want to have to wait until she's back in town to find out. I suppose we could check with the rest of the radio staff, maybe one of them will know. I'm thinking we should start with the manager, and the owner as well, and maybe we can move on from there."

"Oh! The Burbans!"

"Do you know them?"

"Only by name. Lianna Burban is a sponsor for a lot of local artists, and that includes the radio station. She does lots of other stuff too, though, like, oh, she pays for the Closefield Music and Arts Festival every year. She's also, like, eighty."

"Do you know where I could find her?"

"She's pretty reclusive. Doesn't show up in public much. It's her niece, Brittany, I think her name is, who does most of the actual work. Brittany's the one who manages the station. I tried to get into contact with her a couple weeks ago, but she kept dodging me."

"Same here," Ben said, taking off his glasses and leaning back in his nice padded leather office chair. "So how do we find them?"

Julie sat back and chewed her lip for a moment. Then she grabbed her laptop from her bag and started typing hurriedly. Ben noticed that she was a very aggressive typer. Her keys rattled like a snare drum as she searched for something she hadn't felt the need to explain.

The snare drum ceased.

"Got it. They're supposed to appear at a gala this Sunday, both of them. It's in support of local artists and stuff. Lianna's even slotted to give a speech," Julie said, showing Ben her laptop, which was open to the information page for the event. Ben's elation was cut short by the banner at the bottom of the page, which read 'Sold Out.'

"We need to go there," Ben said, and then added "Who're you calling?" because Julie had whipped her cell phone out of her pocket.

"See, with events like this, they give out free tickets to some of the local artists," Julie said, as she dialed a number. She raised a hand to silence Ben as the call was picked up.

"Hey, this is Trip."

"Trip, It's Julie. Look, I was wondering if you had tickets to the gala on Sunday?"

"Yeah, I have them. I was going to give them to Jake and Marvin, since Annie and I can't go because of the concert and all, but their mother is in town. Why?"

"Can I have them?"

"What the hell for?"

"Just for work," Julie said.

"Wait, you found a job? That's great news!"

Julie quickly changed the topic. "Yeah, okay, can I have the tickets?"

"I'll leave 'em on your bed."

"Great, Trip. You're the best. See ya."

"Bye."

Julie hung up before Trip could say anything else and looked up at Ben. He was giving her a strange look.

"So you haven't told your family about your current job?" Ben asked.

"No. And I'm not going to," Julie said, looking down at her hands. Ben was still giving her that look. "Look, if I tell Trip, then he goes and tells Mom and Dad, and if Dad finds out, he'll be pissed. Really pissed. Actually, pissed doesn't even begin to cover it. Especially because I'm working with you," Julie said angrily.

It was Ben's turn to look away, turning his eyes past Julie to the Friday afternoon traffic going back and forth on the street beyond the window. "I'm sorry. I don't want to come between you and your family."

"This is my choice. Mine and mine alone."

Ben nodded. "I understand."

"Yeah, you do. I know Dad does too, which is what ticks me off so much, because he knows what it's like to have this… Calling? Purpose? Obsession? Whatever you want to call it," Julie said. "Sorry. I shouldn't use you like a discount therapist."

Ben sighed. "Just get back to work. Nice job on the tickets."

"Right," Julie said. "Uh… What am I supposed to be doing, exactly?"

"Get me as much as you can on Lianna and Brittany Burban. Especially if either of them had a personal connection with Caleb, beyond music, that is. That way I'll—we'll—know what questions to ask when we meet them."

"Well, you won't have to bother getting an alibi from either of them. Brittany was at a gallery opening that night. Lianna was there too, but then she passed out and spent the rest of the night and all the next day in the hospital."

Ben nodded. The rest of the afternoon passed in a comfortable silence. Julie sat sideways in the armchair with her legs draped over the arm and her laptop poised on her knees, while she scribbled down bits of information into a legal pad she'd borrowed from him. Ben stayed at his desk, except for the occasional trip to the outer office for a cup of coffee from the dinged up old coffee maker that made strange gurgling noises.

Ben came back into the office and sat back at his desk. Though he would much rather have continued to study Caleb Fredrick's life, he had other cases to work on.

He didn't realize how much time had passed until he heard Julie pointedly clear her throat.

"Ahem."

Ben looked up and realized that Julie was standing in front of his desk, wearing her coat and with her bag slung over her shoulder. She slid the borrowed legal pad across the desk to him.

"That's everything I could find off the internet. I tried to write as legibly as I could."

Ben looked at her notes and was gratified to see that he could read them with only a slight headache.

"Thank you. I'll see you Sunday?"

"Yeah. I'll meet you here?"

"Works for me."

Come Sunday evening, Ben was sitting at home at the kitchen table, which often ended up doubling as a home office for him and Lila, reviewing the notes Julie had made. He looked up when he heard the soft padding of Lila's fuzzy-sock-covered feet on the wood floor.

"You look spiffy," she said, leaning over to adjust Ben's tie. Ben put the legal pad down and stood up, picking a cat hair off of his best suit, a neat double-breasted affair in a fine dark-gray fabric.

"Spiffy?" he asked, raising an eyebrow, as went over to the cabinets in search of a lint roller.

"It's what my aunt always said. Aunt Madeleine. It was always "spiffy" with her. Do you know what time you'll be getting back?"

Ben sighed. He wished he did. He wished, suddenly, that he could stay here, with Lila. They could watch The Chronicles of Myst: Episode 3: The Heir of Argentem and eat mediocre Italian food. Instead, he would be socializing with people he hardly knew, trying to coax information out of them, and surviving off of tiny hors d'oeuvres for food. "Not exactly, but I probably won't be home until after midnight. I'll keep you updated."

"Okay. And there'll be food there?"

"I'll be fine," Ben said, though he realized as he said it that it wasn't a proper answer. He finally found a lint-roller, hiding behind the emergency bin of flashlights and a ziplock bag of loose batteries. "I'd best be leaving soon, I've got to pick Julie up along the way."

Julie was waiting for Ben on the office steps. She was wearing a long glittering black dress. Her hair had been done up in an elaborate bun, and she was wearing bright red lipstick. She had silver earrings—Ben didn't know she even had pierced ears—and a matching silver necklace. Instead of her large leather messenger bag, she carried an elegant silver purse, and she was wearing heels—four-inch stilettos—which boosted her height. Ben was relieved to see that she was at least still wearing her bulky black coat, though she had it draped over her shoulders in a way that almost seemed classy.

"Spiffy," Ben said, as Julie climbed into the car.

"Spiffy?"

"Never mind."

The radio played classical music as they drove to the venue.

"The website said parking's in the back," Julie said, when they saw the glowing lights of the hotel. They parked and got out. Julie threw her coat into the car before she closed the door, completing the image of the worldly sophisticate, an image that was then ruined by the clumsiness with which she dug through her purse to find the tickets. She handed one to Ben as they walked through the large glass doors and into the gala.

The high ceiling was hung with glittering chandeliers. Quiet music played softly from hidden speakers. A small stage, elegantly draped in blue and white fabric, had been set up against the far wall. Waiters in navy blue vests milled about, carrying trays laden with champagne and appetizers. Men and women, mostly in their 50s or older, dressed in fine clothing and jewelry, talked amongst themselves. Ben even spied a couple members of the city council in a clump of people to their left.

"It's not particularly… artsy," Ben said, as he took in the scene.

"The main purpose of events like this is to raise funds, so it's mostly the big donors who are invited. Local artists too, though," Julie said, accepting a mini quiche from a waiter and downing it in one bite as she gestured with her free hand toward a clump of younger people who were all standing together toward the back of the room. Their ill-fitting borrowed suits and tuxedos, rumpled hair, and lack of accompanying bling set them apart from the wealthy patrons all around them.

"Have you been to one of these before?" Ben asked.

"Not this one, specifically, but events like it. Don't worry, it's not all small talk and speeches. There should be an artists' showcase somewhere around here, and some of the local bands will probably play a set or two."

"I'm going to find Lianna," Ben said.

"She's over there," Julie said, pointing to where an old woman stood amidst a group of slightly younger people. "Probably Brittany too. But you might want to wait until after her speech. Then you'll have a better idea of her."

"You're right," Ben agreed with a sigh. "But what do we do in the meantime?"

Julie shrugged and downed another mini quiche. Ben figured that if he let her, she'd probably eat them all. Beside, he wanted to find somewhere somewhat entertaining so that he didn't fall asleep before he had a chance to meet Lianna and Brittany.

"Let's go find the art showcase thing," Ben suggested at last.

They followed a trickle of people through a door off to the right. That brought them into a short but painfully narrow hallway, past the marked signs for the bathrooms, and out into a small gallery.

The sheer variety of the artwork stole Julie's breath away. Photographs, sketches, sculptures, one or two wood carvings, portraits, oil paintings, watercolors, and even, in a far corner, what looked like a framed page from a comic book. Here the volume was hushed, and the mood was more relaxed. Maybe it was the softer lighting, or the padded benches set at intervals along the wall, but whatever the case, Julie felt far more comfortable in here than she had in the oversized ballroom.

"Hey! This is one of Trip's!" Julie said, noticing a watercolor in her brother's typical style. It showed a man sitting under a tree with a guitar. The label stuck under the framed piece read 'The Musician. Artist: Richard Bernard.'

"I didn't know your brother did art," Ben said. "It's not bad."

"Yeah, he does watercolors and sketches. Charcoals, too, though not as much. Usually music stuff. A few of the local bands use him for their album covers."

"Cool," Ben said, leaning closer to get a better look at the painting. The man holding the guitar looked like he was deep in his own thoughts. His head was bent and his face was cast in shadow, but still, it was plain that he was thinking about something.

Ben looked up and spied a familiar dark-haired figure sitting on one of the padded benches across the room.

He turned to Julie, who was still examining her brother's painting. "Is that Luke Sebastian?"

"In the painting? No, the hair is too light."

"No, not in the painting, over there, look,"

Julie looked up, her gaze following Ben's as he nodded his head toward the man.

"I'm going to talk to him," Julie announced, and then, before Ben could stop her, she was off, weaving through the crowd until she stood above Luke.

"Luke? It's Julie. Remember? We met at the Palatine a couple days ago."

Luke looked up at her. His pale blue eyes were bloodshot.

"You're the detective girl," he said after a moment.

"Yeah, that's me. I didn't know you would be here."

"Caleb was s'posed to DJ here, did you know that?" Luke asked.

"No, I didn't," Julie said, sitting down on the bench next to him. "I know how hard this must be for you, your friend dying, I mean." Julie tried to sound as sympathetic as she could. It sounded forced and wrong to her, but it seemed to work for Luke.

Luke shook his head blearily. "It's not the first time."

"What do you mean?"

"My brother. Danny. He was twelve," Luke said, tilting his head back so that it rested against the wall.

"That must have been very hard for you. And your family," Julie said. She hesitated for a moment and then awkwardly laid a stiff hand on Luke's shoulder. She immediately regretted it. She'd thought it would be a nice gesture, but it just turned out weird, and she quickly dropped her hand to her lap. Luke didn't seem to notice.

"Do you want to grab a drink?" he asked.

"What, now?"

"It's an open bar here."

Julie thought about it. "Yeah, I'll be with you in a moment, okay?" she said at last, and then she went back to find Ben.

"Luke said Caleb was supposed to DJ here tonight," Julie told Ben, once she'd finally tracked him down. He had been skulking in the shadows of the hallway, trying to be as inconspicuous as possible in the hopes that no one would engage him in conversation unless he wanted them to.

"Well, that's something," Ben said, his brow furrowed.

"Yeah. I don't know if that's something you're going to want to ask Lianna about, or not."

Ben hadn't missed her use of the singular "you" as opposed to "we." "And what are you going to be doing? While I'm talking to Lianna?"

"I'm going to talk with Luke. He's a wreck. This stuff with Caleb, it's dredged up something from his past, I think... Did you know his brother died when he was a kid?"

"I didn't," Ben said. "He told you that?"

"Yeah, and I'm going to see what more I can find out. And right now he's emotional and I think a bit drunk. If he's hiding anything about Caleb, now's the best chance I have to find out what," Julie said. Ben sighed.

"Fine."

"See you, then," Julie said, and then she dodged and weaved through the crowd to meet Luke.

CHAPTER 6:
Champagne and Small Talk

Luke was gone by the time Julie got back and so she was left to find the bar herself. She was about to give up and ask a waiter for directions when she spotted it across the room, tucked away in a slight alcove. Luke was sitting on a bar stool, absentmindedly running his finger around the rim of his glass.

"Hi," Julie said, as she pulled up a seat next to him. As soon as she was seated, she eased out of her four-inch heels and fought the urge to start massaging her aching feet.

"Hey," Luke said, without looking up from his half-empty glass. The jacket of his tuxedo was too small, and the cuffs of his shirt were poking out.

"So, how long had you known Caleb?" Julie asked, trying to make it sound as casual and conversational as possible, which wasn't particularly easy, because the second she started thinking about acting casual, she completely forgot what casual was supposed to look like.

Luke exhaled forcefully, almost a snort. "Caleb and Cameron and Danny. Man, they were three of a kind. Class clowns, you know the type, always getting into all sorts of trouble, and always seeming to get out of it without a scratch," he said with a smile, but then his eyes darkened. "And then one day, Danny went poof and vanished like some cheap magician's trick, and it was just Cal and Cam."

"And you?" Julie asked.

"They'd let me tag along sometimes, when we were younger, when Danny was still there, I mean. I always thought Caleb liked me a bit better then Cam did, at least at first, but as time passed… With Danny gone, they let me come on more and more of their little adventures. Well, long story short, by the time we were all in high school, I'd just… fallen right into Danny's place, I guess. One brother swapped for another, and that was that."

"It's impressive that you've stayed so close for so long. I don't think I've talked to my high school friends in years," Julie said. Luke gulped down the rest of his drink and ordered another.

"Yeah, well, we all loved music, didn't we? Danny too, in his own way. So we all got similar enough jobs, stayed in the industry. I do my thing, and Cam works in music engineering. He's real smart with that tech stuff, got a master's degree and everything. And Caleb, obviously. Caleb just loved all of it. He even tried his hand at songwriting for a while, but he didn't really have the patience for it. Kinda like Danny. You know, Danny, he… He was always singing these little songs he'd made up, had a real nice voice, but when our parents signed him up for music lessons, he was always slacking, flat-out refused to practice…" Luke seemed to realize how much he'd been talking and trailed off. For a moment, he sat completely still, then he shook his head, like a dog shaking off water, blinked, and looked up at Julie.

"But even beyond that, I mean, there was this, like, unspoken bond, between Caleb and Cameron, at least. And Caleb was always good about reaching out and checking in on his friends, making time for them, you know, that sort of thing. So even when we went off to college, we stayed close, and then we all moved back here."

At some point while Luke had been talking, the bartender had set his drink down on a blue paper cocktail napkin in front of him, without either Luke or Julie noticing. Now Luke eyed the drink, trying to remember why it was there, before he took a large gulp of it and sat back in his stool.

While Luke was talking, Lianna Burban had been slowly climbing the steps to the stage, assisted by a middle-aged woman Ben assumed was Brittany. Ben emerged from the shadows of the hallway to get a better look at them. Lianna was small in build, with short gray-white hair. She was wearing a bright red dress covered in frills and sequins, which Ben thought slightly garish. She leaned on a black cane for support. The spotlight glinted off the silver knob that topped it. She reached out to adjust the microphone set in the mic stand and an unearthly screech of feedback attacked Ben's ears. Instead of covering them, as many in the audience had, Ben took the opportunity to pull a small notebook and a pen from an inside pocket of his coat and held them at the ready.

"Hello? Is this thing working?" Lianna asked. Fortunately for the eardrums of everyone involved, there was no feedback this time. "Good. I am so honored to be here today, in front of all of you. It is truly amazing that so many people have volunteered their time and come together in support of the arts, which make life that much more meaningful.

"However, it would be amiss if I did not address the recent tragic events. Every year, a few of our number may leave us, but there is one absence that is particularly notable this year. I am, of course, referring to Caleb Fredrick, who many of you may have instead known as DJ Cal-F. Were it not for his sudden and tragic death, he would have been here tonight, showcasing his skills for all of you. Five percent of tonight's proceeds will go to supporting his family, as a show of our gratitude for all that he has given this community."

Lianna paused for a moment then, and Ben took the opportunity to catch up on his jottings.

"However, on the topic of tonight's proceeds, I am pleased, thrilled, in fact, to announce that we have made over 400,000 dollars, which is a new record high—" Lianna was cut off by a smattering of applause and one or two cheers from the younger guests.

"Yes, yes. We've come a very long way from the first of these little gatherings. I remember the night well. It was held in a high school gymnasium, and there were maybe forty people in attendance, all told. And the food was atrocious! That tiny little gathering has grown and grown before my very eyes, I mean, it's remarkable! I'm so grateful that so many of you have come out here tonight in order to support our local artistic endeavors."

Sensing that she'd come to the end of the relevant portion of her speech, Ben ceased copying down her every word. The rest of her talk was dedicated to thanking the most significant of the donors. Ben dutifully copied down their names in his notebook, but he soon stopped listening to everything else Lianna was saying, as the expressions of gratitude grew increasingly repetitive.

At last, when Ben thought he might genuinely fall asleep standing if he had to hear about another "very generous donation" from another prominent member of society, he heard the telltale slowing of tempo and concluding words that signaled the speech coming to an end. Lianna descended the steps to a genuinely enthusiastic burst of applause, assisted again by the woman Ben assumed was Brittany. Ben started to make his way over to them, but he paused to allow some of the crowd that had gathered around them to dissipate.

Finally, he could wait no longer. "Ms. Burban? I was wondering if you could spare a moment of your time? I'm a private detective, I'm investigating the death of Caleb Fredrick."

The middle-aged woman inserted herself between them and drew herself up to her full height, which wasn't quite enough to reach Ben's shoulder. She wore a teal dress in a hideous gauzy fabric and her hair was a definitely-artificial platinum blonde.

"Ms. Burban is not to be bothered with such macabre matters," she said. Her voice was high-pitched and nasally. She had a narrow, almost pinched-looking face, and her nose was small, delicate, and pointed up in the air in an expression of effortless superiority.

"And who are you to speak for her?" Ben asked, though he had a very good idea.

"I'm her niece. Brittany. I've heard those messages you've left on my voicemail, you might as well save your time and your breath. Neither of us have any intention of giving gossip mongers like you any information."

"Oh, save your own breath, Brittany," Lianna said, stepping past the younger woman and nudging her away. Lianna's un-amplified voice was raspy with age, but by no means weak or frail.

"Auntie, I—"

"You haven't even met the man, and yet you've already made up your mind about him! I suppose it's a bit late in life for you to have an open mind, but would it kill you to keep the door ajar?"

"I don't think you should—"

"I know what you think, but you do not think for me. If you're not going to play nice, then go."

Brittany opened and closed her mouth without a sound. Lianna made a shooing gesture. Brittany's eyes went wide, and Ben wondered if she'd protest, but instead she turned on her heel and stalked off to sit with a tall gray-haired plain-faced man who might have been her husband. Lianna took Ben by the arm in a surprisingly firm grip and steered him away towards the gallery. It was completely deserted now. It seemed that, after leaving to watch the speech, everyone had decided to stay in the main ballroom. Ben and Lianna sat down on a bench by a statue of a rearing stallion.

"Now, if you could please tell me who you are, and who hired you," Liannaaid, once she was settled on the padded bench with her cane poised delicately in front of her. It was phrased politely, but it was quite obviously a command.

"I'm Benjamin Clydesdale, Sydney Fredrick hired me. Caleb's wife. She's disappointed in the way the police investigation has dragged."

"I know who Sydney is, I was the one who introduced them. I'm glad she hired you, someone ought to take a good look at this case. Police blathering on about a robbery, which doesn't make a lick of sense. Why steal a wallet, and nothing else? And kill a man over it, too!"

"Then what do you think happened?"

Lianna's wrinkled face twisted up in the ghost of a smile. "That's your job, I believe," she said, with the barest hint of a throaty chuckle. "I wouldn't know much about that."

"How well did you know Caleb?"

"Oh, fairly well, I suppose, as well as I know anyone these days, except for Brittany, who I sometimes think perhaps I know a bit too well. I was the one who encouraged Caleb to apply his talents on the radio. Before that it was all high school proms and the occasional sweet sixteen," Lianna said. She pulled her wallet from her purse and withdrew a shabby old polaroid which she handed to Ben. The photo showed Caleb, Sydney, Lianna, Brittany, and Cameron Little all sitting at a restaurant together.

"Why's Cameron Little in this picture?"

"Who? Oh, the curly-haired boy. He was there with Clarissa, they've been dating for some time now. Clarissa's the one who took the photo. Good girl, Clarissa. She just aired the thousandth episode of her radio show. Same night that Caleb died, as a matter of fact."

"Did Clarissa invite you to her party that night?"

"She invited me, but it was more of a ceremonial extension of courtesy than a proper invitation. We both knew that it wasn't really my scene. I thought about going to drop by, just for a few minutes, but in the end, I wasn't able to go at all. Minor medical emergency. I don't mean to be rude, young man, but I really ought to be getting back."

"One last question. Caleb's flash drive. Do you know anything about it?"

"What flash drive?"

"Never mind," Ben said, drawing out his business cards and flipping through the stack to the middle, where the cards were somewhat crisp. He drew out the cleanest of these and handed it to Lianna.

"If you think of anything else," Ben said, as he helped her to her feet. She thanked him and vanished into the crowd. Then Ben went off in search of Julie.

As it turned out, she found him first. He saw her coming toward him, holding her skirts up so that she could walk without tripping over her hem.

"Did you get anything useful?" she asked, when she was within speaking range.

"So so. You?"

"Luke was focused more on Danny than on Caleb, but I did learn that Caleb was Danny's friend before he was Luke's. Same with Cameron. When Danny died, Luke sort of took his place in the group, at least, that's how Luke sees it."

"What actually happened to Danny?" Ben asked, because something about the name was ringing a faint bell in the back of his mind.

"Luke didn't say, except that whatever it was, it happened quite suddenly. He talked about Danny 'going poof' so it doesn't sound like this was an illness. Maybe a car crash? That'd be my bet, but I really don't know. And Luke was pretty young at the time, so if it was a longer illness sort of thing, it's very possible he was sheltered from it, until it got really bad, anyway."

"So your answer is that you don't know," Ben said. He was sure he'd heard the name before, and it had been important, but he couldn't quite place it.

"If we go back to the office tonight, we could do some digging," Julie said, stifling a yawn.

"No. It's late. We'll regroup in the morning."

CHAPTER 7:
The Disappearance of Danny Sebastian

Despite what amounted to a meager four hours of rest, after the time it took to explain herself to Trip and then settle her mind enough to be able to fall asleep, Julie showed up on Ben's office doorstep looking neat and put-together, more so, in fact, than Ben had ever seen her look before. Well, she'd looked neat and put-together at the gala, but that had been different, a child in a costume rather than a representation of her true self. Today, however, her hair was brushed and braided and she was wearing a clean sweater over a pair of new jeans.

Ben unlocked the door to let her in, resolving as he did so to give her a spare key, and knowing he'd probably forget. He always left his door locked between the time he arrived and the time he opened up for clients, but that meant that every time he saw Julie, or rather, heard her come clomping up the stone steps, he had to get up and let her in.

"Good morning," Julie said, when he opened the door, looking and sounding far more chipper than Ben felt. He'd had the nightmares again the night before, they'd woken him up and he'd been unable to fall asleep afterward. To the best of his calculations, he'd gotten maybe two hours of sleep. Not enough.

"Morning," he said, feeling unable to add the qualifier "good." He wanted a proper cup of coffee, not the tar-like stuff the ancient coffee maker spat out.

Then, miracle of miracles, Julie whipped a coffee cup from behind her back.

"There's a coffee place on my way here, thought that it'd be nice, after such a late night last night. I already drank mine."

Indeed, when she handed him the tall paper cup and walked past him into the office, he could still smell the coffee on her breath.

She flopped down in the armchair and pulled her laptop from her bag.

"You're looking for information on Danny?" Ben asked. Julie nodded.

"Maybe it's nothing, but, I don't know, it sort of feels important, don't you think?"

Ben nodded and took a sip of his coffee. It wasn't perfect, but it was enough to lighten his mood significantly. "I know. Just be careful that you don't get distracted."

"Yeah, yeah," Julie said, waving one hand dismissively as her other flew over the keyboard. For a few minutes, she was absorbed, keys clicking rhythmically as she searched for answers while Ben flicked through photos of cheating partners for his other cases. He heard Julie's keyboard go quiet.

"Crap!" she exclaimed, as her formerly-flying fingers fell to her side.

"What is it? What did you find?" Ben asked, looking up from his photographs.

Julie looked up at him. Her big hazel eyes were glinting eagerly. "When Luke said that Danny 'went poof' and 'vanished,' he meant that literally."

"Less cryptic, please," Ben said.

"He's missing. Has been for nineteen years. No one knows what happened to him."

"What?"

Julie showed Ben her laptop. Her screen was occupied by a photo of a missing child flyer for Danny Sebastian. He was small for twelve years, with close-cropped dark hair and a dimple on his left cheek. His wild grin was only slightly marred by a set of braces.

"The way Luke was talking, I thought he was dead," Julie was saying.

"That's Danny Sebastian?" Ben asked, because he recognized the boy in the photograph. "I remember that case, it was local, Trinity Lane, in the suburbs just north of here. The prevailing wisdom was that he'd run away. He'd tried a few times before. I knew I recognized the name!"

Julie's eyes flashed. "What do you remember about the case?"

"Not a whole lot, I didn't have much to do with it, and it was a long time ago anyway. He was young, quite young for a runaway, but that was the route the investigation took. I'm going to call Rosie, I think she was more involved than I was. She'll probably remember a good bit more."

"Rosie? Rosie Robinson?"

"The very same," Ben said, cracking a smile for the first time that day.

Rosie Robinson was one of the oldest police detectives in town. She was a plump, cheerful, and vaguely motherly woman, but to Julie, her most distinctive feature was her narrow so-dark-they-were-almost-black brown eyes. Even behind her trademark red cat-eye glasses, they twinkled with shrewd intelligence. She also had a witty sense of humor.

"God, I haven't thought of her in ages," Julie said.

"Well, she probably remembers the case. If I ask nicely, she might even slip me the file."

Julie nodded. "And I've agreed to meet Luke for lunch, day after tomorrow. I'll see if I can find out more from him," and then she turned her attention back to her laptop, to figure out Danny Sebastian.

They stopped for lunch around noon. By that time, Julie had put together a mental picture of who Danny Sebastian had been. He had won the school spelling bee less than a week before he'd vanished. He'd run away twice before, both times with Caleb and Cameron in tow. He had led his soccer team to league victories on three occasions. He was intelligent, restless, energetic, reckless, and mischievous. In every single photo Julie found, his smile projected an infallible self-confidence.

"That's fine work, but I think now it's time to focus on Caleb again," Ben said, when Julie reported her findings over ham and cheese sandwiches.

"But what if they're connected?" Julie asked, spraying breadcrumbs around the room

Ben's inflection revealed nothing of his own opinion. "Do you think that's a possibility?"

"I… I don't know. I haven't found anything to suggest it, except that I guess they knew each other as kids, but I dunno…"

Ben sighed. "For now, let's try to find Caleb's flash drive. That's got to be a part of it. But if you want to look at Danny's case in your spare time, I'm not going to stop you."

"Who even uses flash drives anymore?" Julie grumbled, but after she'd shoved down the last of her sandwich, she switched over to the line of inquiry Ben had suggested, though it had yielded no results by the time they packed up for the day.

That night, Closefield Springs was hit by a massive snowstorm, one of the worst Julie had ever seen. Snow fell three feet deep and the mountainous drifts that formed were nearly as tall as Ben. Trip had grumbled when he'd seen it, but Julie still held that child-like love of snow, and secretly she was thrilled, though she probably would have been less so had the power—and the heating—gone out. Ben phoned to say not to bother coming into the office, so Julie wrapped herself up in a fluffy blanket and curled up on the couch with a mug of hot cocoa to watch Star Trek.

When it became obvious that the snow wouldn't be cleared away by the next day, Julie texted Luke to postpone their meeting. He didn't really seem to mind.

By Thursday, the streets were cleared, life resumed its normal hectic pace, and Julie found herself trudging, in red rubber boots with three pairs of socks for insulation, down the street to the Palatine for lunch with Luke Sebastian.

She swung open the glass doors to the welcome heat, and immediately spotted Luke. The restaurant was not particularly crowded today, it seemed few people had wanted to brave the outdoors, which, according to Julie's meteorology app, was currently exactly one degree Fahrenheit, with cutthroat winds on top.

Luke looked much happier at the Palatine than he had been at the gala. His layered t-shirts actually fit him, for one, unlike the rumpled tuxedo he'd worn then. Here, surrounded by mildly sticky tables, the smell of good food, and 90s pop music playing quietly over slightly scratchy speakers, he was in his element.

"Hey," he said, when he looked up and saw Julie walking over to him. Julie unwrapped her coat and scarf and hat and double-layered mittens and sat down.

"How are you?" she asked, as she settled into her seat. A waiter came by and set down a glass of water. Julie ordered a ginger ale.

"Passable," Luke said, taking a sip of his beer.

"I've started looking into your brother's disappearance."

Luke looked down. "He's dead. I know it. I can feel it in my gut."

"You don't know that. No one does."

Luke's shoulders might have been trembling. "It's worse this way. There's nothing for us to bury. Nowhere we can go to say goodbye."

"Well, how do you know he's dead, then?" Julie asked.

"Danny was a good kid, okay? I know he tried to run away before, but he always came back. He always came back," Luke said. He looked like he was on the verge of tears, but before they could spill over, the waiter came by with Julie's ginger ale and asked them what they wanted. Julie ordered the "farmhouse" sandwich, which had a fried egg, ham, cheese, and spinach. Luke ordered a BLT. Then the waiter left.

"I'm sorry," Luke muttered, once the waiter was gone. "It's just, all this with Caleb, it's bringing it all back, you know?"

"Sorry," Julie said, because she didn't know what else to say.

Luke met her gaze. His pale blue eyes were rimmed with red. "Not your fault. You didn't kill him. You didn't kill either of them."

"It's not fair you had to go through that twice."

"Things like this, like that, it's like… Like, it changes you, changes your life, puts it all on a different track," Luke said, running a hand through his long dark hair. His elegant musician's fingers were trembling.

"I know."

Luke looked up, surprised, shocked, even. It was not the sort of answer he'd been expecting.

"How do you know?" he asked bluntly.

"I…" Julie tried, but her throat seemed to tighten around the words, holding them back. Luke watched her expectantly. Julie told herself that it was only fair for her to tell him, after she'd dragged up his painful past. She sighed.

"My dad is a cop, a detective, actually, and a good one, too, at least, I think so, but I guess I might be a bit biased. My mom traveled a lot for work; she worked as a stylist for fashion shows, she's retired now, but back then, she was in Paris or London or Rome every other week. The school where my brother and I went was too far away from our house to walk, but it was only a few blocks away from the police station, so what ended up happening a lot was that, after school, we'd walk over there, and sometimes Dad would be free right then to take us home immediately, but sometimes we'd have to wait a bit until he or someone else was free," Julie said. Usually, that someone else had been Rosie, and once or twice, it had actually been Ben, just whoever had twenty minutes to spare.

"And?" Luke prompted, eager for the story to continue.

"One day, I was fifteen, I don't know if that's important, another cop, not my dad, brought this guy in to interview in connection with a murder. The murder of Logan Freeman, if that means anything to you, it's not really relevant, I guess. Well, the guy they were going to interview, Tyler Lotsenberg, he was this part-time drug dealer, and witnesses had seen him possibly dealing to Logan, so they brought him in for questioning—" Julie realized she was getting off track and took a deep breath to reorient herself.

"Anyway, this guy, Tyler, when he came in, he was all hyped up on something, I don't know what, but whatever it was, he wasn't thinking too clearly, or else he'd never have done what he did," Julie said, gripping the table, trying to avoid the flood of memories. She flashed to the crazed look in the man's eyes as he'd lunged and grabbed Ben's gun from the holster…

"He was scared, we learned later that a buddy of his had been the one who'd killed Logan, so I guess he was trying to protect him, and he wasn't thinking straight. He got his hands on an officer's gun, and he pointed it at the closest target, the one who seemed the most helpless, the most vulnerable. Me."

Julie didn't remember feeling anything when the bullet had hit her, the pain had only come later, after she'd collapsed to the floor. She remembered the noise, though, angry yells, scared screams, and then a second crack of a gun firing, this time her father's gun, and, even as the world was going blurry, she remembered seeing Tyler Lotsenberg falling to the floor in front of her, blood leaking from his chest, looking like the petals of a red flower.

"My dad was a better shot than he was. I just have an ugly scar. Tyler Lotsenberg lost his life," Julie finished. Her last memory of that day was also her most clear, lying on the gray carpet in a pool of blood, reaching for the man who'd shot her, who now lay, dying, a few feet away from her. Her fingers had brushed his. She'd been looking into his eyes when they went blank and his soul left him.

"Where'd you get hit?" Luke asked. It was a question Julie got a lot.

"Stomach. Right here," Julie said, tracing the spot where, under her heavy sweater, lay a puckered white scar. "The doctors said I was really lucky. It could have been a lot worse."

Luke gave a low whistle. "Bet that fucked you up real good," he said. Julie had to agree. Regardless of whether he meant mentally or physically, it was a fair assessment.

"Honestly, though," Julie said, after a moment, "the worst part wasn't getting hurt, it was watching the man die, and knowing there was nothing I could do to stop it."

"I'm sorry."

"Not your fault," Julie said, her face twisting into a smile. "You didn't shoot me. You didn't shoot either of us."

Luke laughed at that. "So, what do you want to know?"

"Tell me about Danny. Anything you can remember," Julie said, leaning close. She could almost hear Ben's voice in her ear, telling her to focus on Caleb instead, but she blocked it out.

"He was a nice kid, underneath the clown. I looked up to him, ever since I can remember. He was my big brother, yeah, but it was more than that, he just had this air about him, like he could do anything. Nothing was impossible," Luke said, and he pulled out his phone. "Look, I found some old videos."

He showed Julie the phone. The video had clearly been downloaded off of an old video camera. Julie watched as two boys ran through the woods, the camera following close on their heels.

"I think that's Cameron filming," Luke said.

"C'mon guys!" the boy in front yelled. Even in the grainy video, it was easy to recognize Danny, with his wild grin and flashing blue eyes.

"We're going to climb the biggest tree!" Cameron whisper-shouted for the benefit of the audience.

"Who's going first?" the other boy asked. It was a young Caleb Fredrick. He was slight, smaller, even, than Danny, with long dark hair and big dark eyes, like a puppy's.

Cameron set the camera down on a fallen log and stepped into view. "Not me, that's for sure."

"You guys are chickens," Danny said, and he immediately began to climb, hugging the tree trunk and inching his way up until he could swing from branch to branch. He pulled himself up into a seated position on one of the branches. Caleb and Cameron jumped up and down and alternatively cheered and shrieked with fear. Julie wondered how much of their reactions were for Danny's benefit. He seemed the sort who would enjoy an audience.

Danny let go of the branch so that he hung just by his knees, at least forty feet in the air. Julie felt a thrill of terror, but he didn't fall. Danny's shirt flipped down so that it covered his face, and he whipped it off and let it fall to the ground. He gave a great shout of laughter…

That was all.

"He seems… intense," Julie said.

"He was one of a kind," Luke said, pulling up a photo. The picture showed four young boys standing in front of a rose garden. Julie recognized Danny again, and Luke, who was standing off to the side and only half in the frame. All four boys were clearly dressed for school in pressed shorts and polo shirts or clean t-shirts, and carried large backpacks, with hair neatly combed and faces scrubbed clean, except for Danny, who had somehow managed to get a smudge of dirt on his nose, and whose hair was mussed up so that it resembled a bird's nest. There were grass stains on his knees.

"Could you send that to me?" Julie asked. "The photo, the video, and anything else you have of the three of them."

"Yeah, sure," Luke said, taking another sip of his beer. Remembering Danny had obviously been painful for him. Julie wanted to ask more questions, about the day Danny disappeared, but she didn't want to push him, he looked like he was on the brink of tears. The waiter came by with their sandwiches, and Julie and Luke talked about lighter things.

"I know he wasn't perfect," Luke said, while they were waiting for the waiter to come back with the check and Julie's credit card. Somehow Julie knew they were talking about Danny again.

Julie shrugged. "No one is."

"Yeah, I guess. I mean, Danny could be egotistical, and self-centered sometimes, but he was still a good person. Real solid, you know? Like, he was real. There was a side to him, a more sensitive kind of side, it didn't come out very often, but it was there. But most of the time, he was a clown."

"I understand," Julie said. "Thank you, Luke. You've been a great help. If you think of anything else, call me. Or…" Julie hesitated. "Or if you just want someone to talk to."

Then she pulled on her coat, and scarf, and hat, and two pairs of gloves, and she walked back to Ben's office to report what she'd learned.

Chapter 8: Secrets and Lies

The very next day, Julie had brunch with Katie. The temperature was about the same, but at least the wind had died down a bit. Julie was able to leave her scarf at home, and only needed one pair of gloves instead of two.

They met at a café about halfway between Katie's apartment and Ben's office. It was the sort of place Julie probably wouldn't have gone to on her own. She was greeted, as she walked in, by sappy love songs playing over the speakers and the scent of rose petals and nutmeg, and every table had a crisp pink tablecloth that reminded Julie of the furniture in a doll house, but when Julie saw the pancakes on the menu, it was instantly redeemed.

Katie spent the first ten minutes going on and on about a boutique she'd found downtown.

"And all their stuff is from local shops, so, like, yay small business. We should go some time, there's that lovely coffee shop nearby, we can make a date of it," Katie was saying.

"Uh-huh."

Katie went on. "They have some lovely winter coats there, too. You could use a new coat, you've been wearing that big black one since college."

Between the massive stack of pancakes in front of her, Caleb Fredrick, and Danny Sebastian, Julie's mind didn't really have enough cloud space left over to pay attention to what Katie was saying. Even the dig at Julie's beloved coat went all but unnoticed.

"Well, it's all right if you're too busy, I heard you finally got a new job, at least, that's what Trip said when I called looking for you last Sunday, he said you were out at work, except that was at 1:00 in the morning… Say, you haven't become a stripper or something, have you? What's your stripper name?"

"I'm not a stripper."

"Well then, what? C'mon, Jules, I'm dying to know. Tell me. Tell meeee," Katie begged, sticking out her lower pink glossy lip in a pathetic pout.

"I…" Julie stuttered. Katie was the biggest gossip she knew. Any information she found out would be common knowledge by the end of the week.

"Tell me!" Katie demanded. "Or else I'll tell everyone that you're a stripper."

Katie sank back in her seat with a self-satisfied smirk. She knew she had backed Julie into a corner.

"I've joined a private detective agency," Julie said with a wince.

"A what?!"

"You heard me. I got offered a job, and I took it."

"But what did your dad say? With your history and all… What were you thinking?" Katie asked, her blue eyes wide, her normal shallow façade dropped.

"My dad doesn't know, no one does. This is what I've always wanted to do, Kate."

"I know you wanted it when you were younger, before…" Katie's voice trailed off.

"Before I got shot, you mean?" Julie asked. The conversation with Luke the day before had torn down her normal reservations regarding the Incident. She met Katie's eyes with a brazenness that bordered on recklessness. "Before I watched a man die?"

Katie dropped her gaze to the pink and white checkered tablecloth. "You know what I mean, Jules," she said, her voice gentle, soothing.

Rather than having the calming effect she'd intended, this only fanned the flames of Julie's anger.

"Cops get hurt and keep going all the time, it's part of the job," Julie said, fighting to keep her voice under control.

"But you're not a cop, Julie. You're still… I mean you always were…." Katie stuttered to a halt.

"I'm still what?" Julie asked, her voice dangerously icy. "What, Katie?"

"Still a kid playing pretend," Katie whispered.

"Fuck you."

"What?"

"You heard me, Kate. Fuck off," Julie said, picking up her coat and bag. It would take too long to shove on her gloves and hat, so she stuffed them into her pockets instead. She grabbed a twenty-dollar bill from her bag and slapped it down on the table with a thud that rang throughout the café. Then she stormed out into the cold. She couldn't admit to herself that the reason Katie's comment had cut so deep was because, deep down, she knew it was true.

Ben could see that Julie was angry about something when she came into the office and accidentally slammed the door behind her. He looked up.

"You look freezing," he said, because Julie was shivering violently. Her coat hadn't been buttoned properly, and when she drew her hands out of her pockets, he could see that they were bare.

"I'm fine," she said. It had only been a short walk, and she'd done it quickly. Still, she didn't think she could have stood another few minutes.

Ben got Julie a mug of hot coffee and the blanket he kept under his desk for those occasional nights when he crashed on the office couch. On nights when Lila was out of town for work, it was so easy to get lost in his work and lose track of time.

He would have liked to stay and find out what had gotten Julie in such a mood, but he had a meeting with Rosie Robinson in a few minutes. Still, he cast a worried look at Julie over his shoulder as he left.

When he came back, Julie was looking much warmer and excited instead of agitated.

"What did Rosie say?" she demanded before he'd even had a chance to get his coat off.

"In a minute," Ben said, as he set his bag down on his desk. Julie stood in front of him, almost bouncing up and down in her eagerness. Ben was reminded of a young child at Christmas. He pulled a legal pad from his bag and glanced down at it.

"Let's start at the beginning," he told Julie, who immediately took a dry-erase marker and started a second timeline on the whiteboard underneath the one marking Caleb's death. Ben handed her a printed-out photograph of Danny, which she pinned to the board with a magnet next to the timeline.

"When did he disappear?" Julie asked.

"Danny Sebastian disappeared the night of November 7, 2001."

Julie made a mark toward the beginning of the line and motioned for Ben to continue.

"He vanished in the middle of the night, during a camping trip with Cameron Little and Caleb Fredrick. The last time they claim to have seen him was around 11:30, when they went to sleep. When they woke up, around 6:00 or 6:30, he and his things were gone. The last time anyone beside Cameron or Caleb saw him was at 3:00 pm, when all three boys went into the woods behind the Sebastian residence for their camping trip. At 8:00 that morning, after searching the woods for Danny, Cameron and Caleb returned in a panic and notified the parents, who notified the police. The general consensus was that he ran away."

"But the times he ran away before, he brought Caleb and Cameron with him, so why leave them behind this time?" Julie asked, turning from the whiteboard to Ben. Her eyes were gleaming again.

Ben shrugged. "Not sure. But you don't seem to think that he ran away at all."

"Luke doesn't think so. He's sure Danny's dead."

"I didn't ask what Luke thinks, I asked what you think," Ben said patiently.

"I agree with him. Danny ran away before, but never for long, and always with Caleb and Cameron. What did the boys say at the time?"

"They said the evening before had been mostly normal. They'd climbed trees, played in the creek, had sword fights with sticks, until over s'mores, Danny mentioned the idea of leaving town. But they said that they didn't think much of it, until they woke up and he was gone. They went looking for him and found nothing before going back home and getting the grown-ups involved. The police were notified, but they assumed, based on Caleb and Cameron's testimony and the fact that he'd run away before, that he'd run away again, and so that was the angle their investigation took."

"So what do you think?" Julie asked, when her notes had caught up. "Runaway, or dead?"

"The two are not mutually exclusive. Maybe he tried to run away and got eaten by a grizzly bear," Ben said, the corner of his mouth twitching.

Julie bit her lip. "There aren't a whole lot of grizzly bears in Closefield Springs. A black bear, maybe. But all we really know is that now, almost twenty years later, his best friend turned up with a knife planted in his back. And that makes his disappearance potentially very sketch."

Ben raised an eyebrow. "Sketch?"

"Suspicious. Weird. Fishy."

"There aren't a whole lot of fish in Closefield Springs, either," Ben said, fighting a grin. Julie looked at him for a second and then burst out laughing. Ben watched her for a moment, and then he couldn't help himself anymore, and he started laughing too, the both of them almost bent double with mirth as the photographs of two young men, one dead and one missing, watched on from the whiteboard.

Eventually Julie recovered her breath. "I needed that."

"Yeah. Me, too," Ben said.

They took a short break having made very little progress, but with their respective moods significantly lightened.

Julie left the inner office for her "break" to get away from the murder board. She sat perched on the large desk in the outer office, the one occasionally occupied by secretaries, when Ben could afford them. She swung her legs back and forth, blowing bubbles of artificial-cough-syrup-grape-flavored gum and listening to punk rock over a pair of bright neon pink headphones, which she'd purchased out of a bargain bin at Walmart.

Ben's method of head-clearing involved far less eardrum damage and far more frozen fingers. He went for a walk around the block, head bowed against the wind, a blue hand-knitted scarf (a gift from Lila) wrapped around his neck, mouth, nose, and ears.

He turned the last corner and trotted the last few steps and up the stairs. He threw open the door and shut it quickly behind him. Sometime in the last hour, that horrible biting wind had decided to come back, and he had some trouble getting the door closed. Julie pulled off her headphones and spat her gum into the wastepaper basket, where it stuck like a giant purple booger in the plastic bag lining.

"Hi," Julie said, as she hopped down from the desk and shoved her headphones into her messenger bag.

"Hey," Ben returned, opening the door to the inner office. Julie followed him in and went to her armchair. She stretched, cat-like, and then pointed a lazy finger at the board.

"So what's our verdict, then? Is Danny's disappearance related to Caleb's death?"

Ben sighed. "Personal opinion or professional opinion?"

"Both, I guess."

Ben took off his wire-rimmed glasses and started cleaning them with his shirt, as he often did when he was thinking.

"I think," he said slowly, picking his words very carefully, "I think it's possible. But for now at least, we need to investigate them as separate."

Julie was not entirely satisfied. "What if the flash drive has something to do with Danny? What if Caleb had been investigating, trying to find Danny, and he recorded everything on the flash drive, but someone wanted Danny to stay missing?"

Ben sighed. "If we discover evidence that that was the case, then you can investigate Danny's disappearance to your heart's content. For now, just comb through the rest of what Rosie gave me. If you see anything you think is related to Caleb's death now, then we can talk. If not, then put it on the back-burner for a while."

"You're the boss," Julie said grumpily. Ben handed her the legal pad lying on his desk.

"That's got everything Rosie told me. It doesn't leave this room, understand? Some of it we're not supposed to have, strictly speaking, but Rosie trusts us."

"Us? You told her I'm working with you?" Julie asked, taking the pad and flipping through it absentmindedly.

"She was thrilled. Said it was about time you got into the game," Ben said.

"Wish Dad saw it that way," Julie grumbled.

"You're a lot like your father, you know. Your eyes gleam the same way when you're looking at something confusing or interesting."

Julie looked down at her hands. Ben thought she might be blushing. "I've got work to do," she said at last.

"Yeah. And when you're done, call around and find out when Alex Harcourt is getting back. We still need to know what the hell was on the flash drive."

"Yessir."

CHAPTER 9:
A Song for Winter

As it happened, Alex returned to Closefield Springs the very next day. On Monday, when they regrouped after the weekend, Ben announced that he would be meeting with Alex alone. Partially because he had a feeling Alex would be a more delicate witness, and he wasn't sure how well Julie would handle that, but also partly because he had another job he needed her to do.

"I want you to go to the radio station and poke around there; who Caleb liked, who Caleb didn't like. And see if you can't talk to Brittany Burban. Just maybe don't tell her you work for me," Ben explained to a hurt Julie.

"I wanted to meet Alex!"

"I know, but I need this done, and Brittany knows who I am already. If she sees me poking around, she'll probably try to throw me off the premises. But she doesn't know you. You'll be able to get in."

"What do I tell them? It sounds like the truth won't exactly fly well."

"You'll figure it out; I believe in you," Ben had told her, and she'd seemed pleased by that. She'd left without a trace of resentment or reluctance.

Now, sitting in front of an empty chair at the Palatine, ten minutes after the agreed-upon meeting time, Ben wondered if it had all been pointless; if Alex Harcourt would show at all. When he'd called, she had agreed readily to the meeting, but she hadn't exactly sounded thrilled about the idea.

He was just about to give up when he saw her passing by the window. She burst in through the door, a small cloud of snow blowing in with her. She looked around for a moment before spotting Ben and hurrying over. She took the seat across from him and slid her lime green coat onto the back of the chair.

Alex was a pale kid, with bright freckles spattered over her nose, even in the dead of winter. Her hair was spiky and dark, but he could see ginger at the roots. The tips had been dyed bright green. Under her coat, she wore torn gray jeans (Ben supposed they might once have been black) and a ragged t-shirt for what Ben thought was a band, though he'd never heard of Murder Rabbit before. Her nose was pierced with an emerald stud.

"Sorry for being late," she said, leaning back in the chair. "My sleep schedule is still all wonky."

"It's not a problem," Ben said. "I understand you've been in Wyoming the last few months?"

"Yeah, with my big brother, you know? It was scary, Cal dying like that," Alex said. Ben noticed her hands were trembling a little. She clenched them into fists and the trembling stopped.

"I understand you're the one who found him?" Ben asked gently.

"Yeah. Man, that was screwed up, he was just lying there, and there was so much blood, and this massive knife in his back…"

"Were you close with Cal?"

"Close-ish, I think. He was a nice guy," Alex said. "He was there if you needed him."

"Did you work for him long?"

"Almost three years? Yeah. I mean, it was part-time at first, while I was finishing high school. Started full-time about a year ago," Alex said, with a nervous glance at Ben's notebook. Ben took the hint and tucked it away in his jacket pocket.

"Is that what you like to do? Music stuff?" Ben asked more conversationally.

"Oh yeah. It's big in my whole family, except my brother, I guess. My parents own Closefield Recording Studio," Alex said.

"Yeah, I've heard of that place," Ben lied. He made a mental note to ask Julie about it later.

Alex nodded. She looked more comfortable, now. The waiter came by, and Ben ordered iced tea and a chicken pot pie. Alex just ordered a salad. And a root beer float, which Ben thought probably went against the purpose of eating a salad, but he didn't comment.

"So you started working at the radio station while you were in high school?" Ben asked, slowly steering the conversation back to Caleb.

"I guess so, I mean, they were the ones who paid me, but really I was working for Caleb. Which also means I'm out of a job, now that he's gone. That's part of why I went to Wyoming. I'm thinking of moving there now. Not sure yet, just thinking," Alex said.

"I see," Ben said, making another mental note.

"What else do you want to know?" Alex asked, taking a sip from her root beer float. Ice cream foam clung to her lips, mingling with her dark purple lipstick, but she didn't seem to notice. "Like, my alibi, and stuff? That's what the cops wanted. And they wanted to hear about the person Caleb was arguing with, but I told them I didn't know who it was."

Ben looked up. "Caleb was arguing with someone before his death?"

"You didn't know?"

"No, I didn't," Ben said. "Why don't you tell me about it?"

"It was at the anniversary party, for the radio station, not Clarissa's thing. It was the fifty-year anniversary of WCSP, back in November, but everyone was too busy then, so we didn't have the celebration until early January. Turned into a sort of New Years thing. Anyway, Lianna held the party at this resort, the Woodsley. Real fancy place. Everyone who worked at the station was there, and their partners, too. Brittany even came, though her husband was in LA, something for work. That was a bit of a surprise, she never comes to those sorts of things. But anyway, my room was next to Caleb and Sydney, and that night, as I was walking past their room, I heard people yelling."

"Could it have been Caleb and Sydney?"

"It couldn't have been Sydney, she was still downstairs, having coffee in the lounge with the other spouses. I was hanging out with them, and then I realized I'd left my phone up in my room, so I went up to get it. It was while I was walking back that I heard the argument. I know one of them was Caleb, but the other person was farther from the door, I couldn't really tell anything, except that they were angry."

"Male? Female?"

"Could have been either, really. It was on the deepish side, so more likely a guy, I guess, but it could have been a deep-voiced woman."

"Did you hear any of what was said?"

"Only Caleb, and only snippets. Something about 'there's nothing you can do to stop me' and then the other guy interrupted. And right at the end he said something like 'the lies have to end.' But everything else was hard to pick out. They were pretty quiet about it, they didn't seem to want other people to hear."

"Did you see who it was, then? Even a glimpse?"

"I think they rushed past me, as I was going down the stairs, but I couldn't see who it was. I'm pretty sure it was them, because they were all panicked, and you would be panicked, wouldn't you, if you'd just been in a fight, but I guess I don't know for sure."

"How couldn't you see?" Ben asked, trying not to betray his frustration. Finally, they had a proper good lead, but it seemed there was no way to follow up on it.

"They were wearing a blue sweatshirt with the hood up, and they were going very fast. At the time I forgot all about it. I went down to the lounge and hung out with Sydney and the other spouses for a while longer, then went back up to bed. And I did tell all of this to the police, and I think they asked around, but they weren't ever able to figure out who it was."

"It's all right. Thanks for telling me," Ben said.

"What else do you want to know? My alibi? I was at the movies, with my parents and a couple of their friends."

"I know. I called your parents a few times to try and find out when you were coming back. Your mother told me," Ben explained.

"Oh. Great."

"There is another thing I want to know, though," Ben said. "I wanted to ask you about Caleb's flash drive."

Alex poked at one of the few remaining sliced strawberries in her salad. "That was our secret, Caleb's and mine. He didn't want anyone else to know about it."

Ben buried his frustration and tried to sound patient. "But Alex, Caleb's dead now. You're not helping him by keeping it a secret. In fact, if Caleb was killed because of whatever is on it, the only person you'd be helping is the person that killed him."

That shook her. "Okay," she said, biting her lip, "See, Caleb had this project, only no one else knew about it, not even Sydney, or Luke, or Cameron, or Brittany, or… You get the idea. He wanted to make a song, see, to express some truth, or whatever. I asked what it was about once, but he got all weird and quiet and wouldn't tell me anything. I didn't dare ask again. I think that's why he asked for an assistant, really, and chose me, because I could help him. I had my parents' studio, he could record stuff in peace without the whole town knowing."

"And this work, this song, it was stored on the flash drive?"

"Yeah, all of it. Lyrics, chords, sheet music, and the actual recording of course. We'd just finished it a week… a week before he died," Alex said, looking down. Ben thought he saw tears brimming in her eyes, but she wiped them away. When she looked up, she was under control again.

"And you're sure no one else knew about it?"

"Positive. We only ever worked on it in my family's studio. My parents knew something was going on, because we kept booking studio time, but they didn't know what. I did all the tech and the mixing myself."

"What about other musicians? Did he hire anyone to play additional instruments?"

"No, it was just us. He sang and played bass, and I did the guitar and the drums and the keyboard."

"Are there copies of the flash drive anywhere? Could I see what was on it?"

Alex hesitated for a moment and then reached into her bag and pulled out a flash drive adorned with sparkly panda stickers. Ben held out his hand. Alex chewed her lip for a moment before reluctantly dropping the flash drive into his palm.

"I don't really need it anymore, anyway. I just carry it around out of habit," Alex said, though she was obviously loathe to part with it.

"Thank you. You've been… phenomenal," Ben said, as he slipped the flash drive into his coat pocket. Alex eyed the pocket for a moment, and Ben feared she would lunge and grab at it rather than see him walk away with it, but then the moment passed, and Ben paid the bill and left the restaurant.

No one noticed Julie as she walked into the front office of the radio station. Even the receptionist, a tiny mouse-like young woman about Julie's age, hardly looked up from her computer. It was far neater than she'd expected, all the furniture was modern and sharp-cornered and the room smelled of lemon-scented cleaning products.

So far unhindered, Julie made her way down the hallway to the break room. As she progressed down the hallway, the mood became increasingly relaxed and the aggressively clean scent was replaced by the smells of fast food and chocolate masking cigarette smoke and just a hint of weed.

Julie came to the doorway to the break room and poked her head inside. This was the room where Caleb had been killed. It didn't look magical, or sinister. There was nothing to properly distinguish it from any of the other break rooms she'd seen over the years. The blue-striped couch didn't quite match the scratched leather armchair, and the wall near the kitchenette sported a cheesy cat calendar. It didn't look like a room in which a man had lost his life.

"Can I help you?" someone asked behind her. Julie jumped, turned, and came face to face with a tall woman of around thirty. She had dark curly hair, a hawkish sort of nose, and wore a pair of skinny jeans with a neat blouse and a pair of large rectangular glasses that made her look vaguely insect-like.

Julie put on a slightly clueless expression. "Maybe. I was wondering what you could tell me about Caleb Fredrick?"

"Why do you want to know?" the woman asked suspiciously.

"I'm a reporter," Julie lied. "I'm doing a piece on Caleb and the radio station for the Closefield Times. Would you be willing to talk? Not just about the murder, but about him, who he was, what sorts of things he did, what sorts of things were bothering him."

It seemed good enough. The woman's gaze went from suspicious to vaguely eager.

"All right. We can talk," she said. "But let's not do it in there. Too much bad energy. I'm Clarissa Byron, by the way. I DJ the slot immediately before Caleb's, and my boyfriend was one of his best friends."

Clarissa led Julie back to the reception room and to the sharp leather furniture set that did not seem like it had been designed for human use. Julie took one of the rigid armchairs, and Clarissa sat on the stiff sofa across from her. Julie took care to keep her knees far away from the very sharp-looking corners of the glass coffee table. The mousy receptionist, who quietly introduced herself as Pippa, brought over two cups of coffee and handed them to Julie and Clarissa.

"What did you say your name was?" Clarissa asked.

"Julie. Julie Bernard," Julie said, after recovering from a sip of coffee so hot it instantly burned her tongue.

"I see. Well, what to say, Caleb was a nice guy."

Julie set the coffee cup down on the table, noticed Clarissa shooting it a look, and then slid a coaster under it, which seemed to be the correct response. "Did he have a lot of friends?"

"Not particularly, but he had a few. He was closest with Alex Harcourt I think, his assistant, and I like to think he counted me as a friend, too. And Cameron, of course, but they've known each other for ages, and Cameron doesn't really work here, he just drops by from time to time to fix the equipment when it gets buggy. It's not that Caleb was mean, or anything, just a bit introverted. Beyond work, there was his wife, obviously, and this other childhood friend of his, Sam, or Mark, something basic like that."

"Luke?"

"Oh yes, Luke, that's it."

"Did anything bother Caleb? That you know of?"

"He was the easy-going sort. Nothing really seemed to bother him, and I don't think he'd have told anyone if it did. He was on the quiet side, and private, too."

Julie was about to ask another question, but a door to the side marked "Manager" swung open, and an angry-looking woman with very artificially blonde hair stepped out.

"Who are you, exactly?" she demanded.

"I'm Julie Bernard, I'm from the Closefield Times—"

"Go away," the woman ordered.

"If I could just ask a few questions—"

"Please just leave us alone," the woman said, her volume increasing slightly with every word.

Julie sighed and stood up. It seemed the interview was coming to an end.

"I'm sorry to have bothered you."

"Sorry? You people, buzzing around like carrion birds. No peace! Sorry, my ass."

Julie muttered another apology and fled.

As she left, she was greeted by a rush of very cold air. Snow was falling again, and the wind had picked up. It would be a long, cold walk back to Ben's office.

"Hey! Detective girl! Want a ride?" someone called. Julie turned and saw a bundled-up Cameron Little coming out of the building she'd just been in. He pointed to his vehicle, a large gray van with a logo of two eighth notes patterned like circuit boards on the side.

"Sure," Julie said. Semi-stranger danger be damned, it was cold out, and the walk back to Ben's office was not appealing.

She climbed into the passenger seat of the van. It was surprisingly clean inside. A little plastic hula dancer stood on the dashboard and jiggled merrily when Cameron turned the van on and backed out the parking space.

"Where to?" Cameron asked, as he nosed out onto the street.

"211 Mountain Avenue."

"I heard Brittany going after you," Cameron said after a moment. Traffic was bad, probably because of the snow, and horns and shouts played background accompaniment to the winter's day.

"So that was Brittany Burban. I figured. She's... a lot."

"Don't mind her, she's just tired of all the people who've been hounding her since Cal died."

"Did they get along? Caleb and Brittany?"

Cameron laughed. "As well as anyone gets along with Brittany. She's got a sharp tongue and she's prone to snap judgments. And she can be elitist, and pretentious, and generally a snob. And her husband might actually be a robot. I do not recommend engaging him in conversation. He hasn't bored anyone to death yet, but it's only a matter of time."

"Guess you don't like them much?"

"Not particularly. But I do respect Brittany. And I'm sure somewhere, under all those layers, there's a human being worth knowing. But I'm not around her enough to try and find it."

"I see," Julie said.

"Man, sometimes I'm glad I don't work at the station," Cameron said after a moment.

"Because of Brittany?"

"In part. But it also seems awful lonely. There's hardly ever any other people there with you. Caleb and Clarissa were friends, and Duke and Brittany get on pretty well. Those are the people I know best, I don't normally do major work or anything during the day. Point is, when I am there, in the middle of the night, it's just you and maybe one other person in the whole building, and you know that almost everyone else in town is fast asleep. It's just… lonely."

A thought occurred to Julie. "Did you do anything there the night Caleb died?"

Cameron shook his head. "No, I was at Clari's party, remember?"

"Right, sorry."

By now they were approaching the turn-off to Ben's street, which involved a rather nasty traffic circle, and the traffic was moving slower than ever. Ahead of them, someone was laying on the horn to no avail. Cameron tapped his fingers along the steering wheel.

"What do you remember of Danny Sebastian?" Julie asked on a whim.

"He ran away," Cameron said. "I know Luke doesn't want to believe it, but Danny ran away. Don't know what happened to him after that."

"Was there something going on in his home life, that would have made him run away?"

"Not really, and I think that was part of the problem. Danny always wanted some sort of adventure, but the place we lived, it was your classic happy little suburb all PTA soccer moms and neighborhood association. Joggers, people out walking their dogs, baseball games in the empty lot on the corner, backyard cookouts. Couldn't have been more perfect and boring if it tried. Danny always seemed to think of it like a trap. I guess he'd just had enough. To be perfectly honest, Cal and I sort of thought the same way, when we were younger, but we grew out of it. Danny didn't."

Finally, the traffic started moving again. Cameron heaved a sigh of relief.

Julie pressed on. "And Luke? I mean, was he the same way?"

"Luke annoyed the heck out of Danny, always trying to tag along, looking up at him like a pathetic little puppy. Deep down, I think Danny cared about him, but he certainly didn't show it very often."

Julie was taken aback. "Luke made it sound like Danny was good to him."

Cameron shook his head. "Nothing but a fantasy. Danny could be downright rude, not just to Luke, but to us, too."

Julie changed the subject. "I met Clarissa today. She's really nice."

"Clari? Yeah. As soon as we get financially stable, we're gonna get married. We both want lots of kids. Neither of us had any siblings growing up, and we don't want our children to be so alone. We're gonna live in a penthouse in a big city, so that we have a view out over town. I've always liked it, up in the air. Like you're flying."

"Oh."

"You have a brother, right? You mentioned him the other day."

"Yeah. Trip."

"Nice."

They turned onto Ben's street and Julie saw the green door.

"This is the place," she said. Cameron stopped the van, and Julie hopped out and sprinted through the wind to the shelter of the office.

Ben was already there when Julie got back.

"How'd it go?"

Julie made a so-so motion with her hand. "I talked with Clarissa Byron for a bit, and then Brittany appeared, and the lie I'd used was that I was from the paper, which she didn't seem to like much, and she kicked me out. I didn't get a chance to ask Clarissa about the flash drive, it was hard to steer the conversation there without sounding too suspicious. But then I ran into Cameron Little as I was coming out, and he gave me a ride back here. I tried to ask a few questions, but I didn't get anything useful. You?"

Ben grinned. "Alex Harcourt was very helpful." Ben pointed to the board, where he'd added what he'd learned.

"Argument at the hotel?" Julie asked. "Caleb had an argument with someone a week before he died?"

"According to Alex. But she couldn't tell us who it was. She saw the person, too, afterward, they ran past her on the stairs, but they were wearing a hoodie. And the only words she picked up were from Caleb. 'The lies have to end,' and 'there's nothing you can do to stop me.'"

"Great. So we know Caleb was arguing with someone, probably the killer, but we don't know who it was."

"Yup."

"Who else was at the resort then? I mean, who else from Caleb's world?"

"The entire radio staff, apparently. And their spouses. There are five different shows that run every day. First, it's this guy, Duke Werkle, but on the radio, he's called The Duke. The morning rush hour slot is covered by two brothers, Steve and Harry Jumper. The lunchtime slot is done by Mary Catherine Roger and Janie Willis. Then it's Clarissa, and then Caleb. Caleb, Janie Willis, and Mary Catherine Roger, and Duke Werkle all have assistants as well. We know Alex, obviously. The assistant for Janie and Mary Catherine works part-time as a receptionist, so you might have met her. But the Duke's assistant is a mystery. He talks about her on the air sometimes, but he never calls her by name, always 'My Duchess.'"

"Are they in love?"

"They act like it, on the air, I don't know if it's real or not. But from some of the things they've said, it sounds like Duchess is married. They've never come out as said it in as many words, but there're hints. Sometimes very strong hints."

"What if Caleb found out who it was? What if he was going to tell Duchess's spouse?"

"Duke was on the air when Caleb was killed, he couldn't have done it."

"Commercial break?"

"Would that give you enough time to go to the break room, find Caleb, and kill him?"

Julie thought about it for a moment. "Depends. The actual station is at the end of the hallway, the break room is about halfway down it. If he ran, that'd be about fifteen seconds, so half an ad, most ad breaks have what, six or seven? Ten maybe? Plus, time to argue, grab the knife, stab Caleb, and hide his body behind the sofa, and then another fifteen seconds back… I think it's possible. Tight, but possible."

"Especially if they didn't argue. If Caleb's back was turned, Duke could have just rushed him before he knew anyone was there," Ben pointed out.

Julie nodded, and added Duke's name to the board.

"Do you want to know what else I got out of Alex?" Ben asked.

"What?"

Ben grinned and held up the flash drive Alex had given him.

Julie's eyes went wide and she gave an excited squeak. "Is that… That's not… It can't be…"

"It's not the flash drive, if that's what you're asking. This was Alex's, but it's a complete copy of Caleb's."

"And you didn't lead with that?" Julie asked, her voice going shrill with frustration, but she was smiling.

"I wanted to get your thoughts on our mystery arguer first. If I'd led with the flash drive, you'd have been distracted all day."

"Have you looked at it yet?" Julie asked, leaning forward to get a better look at the legendary flash drive, as if she could see the contents if she just stared long enough.

"No, I wanted to wait for you. Shall we?"

"Do you really need to ask?" Julie said, jamming the flash drive into her computer violently enough that Ben worried she'd break it.

"It should be the files for some song Caleb was working on," Ben said. "Alex helped him with it, but she said she never knew what the song was about."

"Found the lyrics, let's see…"

"Well?" Ben asked eagerly. "What's it about?"

"Um… not sure really. Want me to read it aloud?"

"Sure."

"Never was much good at poetry recitation," Julie grumbled, but she cleared her throat and began.

"Suburbia and Subarus, childhood incarnate.

Playing little games that never turned out real

One of your little games,

though, turned raw and deep

The world felt the wound

it'd never be the same.

"The river that carried you is carrying me as well

I feel it every time the river swells

After all that's said and done

After all that went so wrong

Under the roses is where you found release"

Julie cleared her throat. "That's the first verse and chorus. Do you want me to go on?"

"Sure. But skip the chorus."

"Mama always raised me

To respect the Holy Trinity

Of Father, Son, and Holy Ghost

That day in our perfect home

I found a new Trinity

Of Hating, Lies and Fear.

"A story with no ending

No conclusion, no resolution

Sometimes that's the way of life

But let this be an ending

A conclusion, a resolution

That doesn't have to be the way of life."

"That it?" Ben asked, when Julie went quiet.

"Yup."

"Thoughts?"

"The song seems to be about growing up, the line between childhood and adulthood. All of the verses have, like, a duality about them, the first half talks about the way things were, the second half the way things are, or will be."

Ben went quiet for a moment before speaking. "Could it be about rape?"

Julie scanned the passage again, her face growing pale. "That would fit," she said after a while. "There's definitely an aspect of violence, that's for certain."

Ben nodded. "But now the real question: is this song the reason Caleb was killed?"

Julie shook her head. "I just don't know. The flash drive was stolen, that would indicate yes, but it could have just been taken as part of his wallet, to make it look like a robbery."

"So yet again, we have a potential lead, but no way to follow it up."

"You could talk to Sydney, she might not have known about the song, but maybe if you show her the lyrics, she'll know what they're about."

"I'm meeting with her tomorrow anyway, I can ask her then. And we can talk to Duke Werkle."

"And ask him what? If he killed Caleb?"

"We'll talk to him like he's a witness, after all, he was in the building the night Caleb died."

"Okay. And if we can steer the conversation toward his Duchess, then all the better," Julie said, sighing and leaning back in her chair. "One question answered, another appears."

CHAPTER 10:
Questions Unanswered

Tuesday morning, Ben arrived to find Julie already at work, sitting in his chair and with her ice-damp sneakers up on his desk. She looked up when he came in and grinned at him sheepishly. Ben glared at her. She sighed and removed her shoes from the desk, leaving a small puddle behind.

"I found the spare key under the mat. That's like using 'password' for your password," Julie said, as she sat down in her own chair.

"Uh-huh," Ben said, taking his seat and wiping up the water with his shirt sleeve. "And what have you spent your time working on? Or were you just here for the free wifi?"

Julie pretended to look hurt. "I'll have you know, I've been researching Duke Werkle. He's thirty-six years old, divorced, and has one kid, Stephen, age five, who lives with his mother in Delaware. Duke started working at the radio station almost fifteen years ago, right out of college, where he majored in economics, but he was a music minor. He's held the same time slot ever since, though he's tried to move it several times, most recently, last December."

"Where'd you get all that?"

"Facebook," Julie said with a shrug. "And Instagram. And Twitter. Social media makes this whole detective thing a lot easier. People are practically investigating themselves!"

"And did any of your research tell you how we're going to talk to him?"

"Rivers Bar and Grill. You know the one? They have that hideous giant plastic pig outside?"

"The barbecue place?"

"That's it. He really likes it there, apparently."

Ben was impressed, but he didn't let it show. "So what? We ambush him there tonight? Seems a little unprofessional."

"But effective. The only real issue is that Rivers is one of those really loud places, which might make it a bit hard to talk properly, but at least we won't be overheard," Julie said, and then she went quiet for a moment and looked down at her shoes.

"What is it?" Ben asked.

"I've trawled through this guy's life so much, I feel like I know him. I mean, I don't really want to, he's kind of a greaseball, but I do. And I feel like I know Danny, too. But Caleb… He's like a blank wall. That doesn't seem fair, exactly. Caleb's the one who's dead, the one we're supposed to know everything about. I did lots of research on him, when I was trying to figure out his death by myself, and still I never really felt like I had a measure of him."

Ben nodded. "Some people keep their secrets close to their chests. Caleb was one of those people."

"But it's our job to find those secrets, and we haven't, not really. I mean, we got the damn flash drive, and we have no idea what that stupid song's about!"

"We will."

Julie didn't seem entirely satisfied with that, and Ben didn't blame her, but she nodded and started writing up what she'd learned about Duke Werkle on their whiteboard.

At 11:45, Ben shooed Julie out of the office. She was supposed to meet Trip and her parents for lunch that day, but she was dragging her feet about it.

"Are you sure you don't need me to stay? There's so much work to do," she said.

"I think I can spare you for an hour or two."

"Positive? I really wouldn't mind, I can text Trip and cancel."

Ben glared at Julie, who sighed and grabbed her coat with the air of a sulky teenager.

Ben was grateful that she was leaving, anyway, he was supposed to meet Sydney, and he wasn't certain enough of Julie's social skills to have her interacting with the grieving widow.

Sydney arrived at 12:30 looking better than she had the last time Ben had seen her, though that wasn't really saying much. The shadows under her eyes were still there, but they were less pronounced now, and she had gone from skeletal to merely skinny.

"You're looking well," Ben said, as she took a seat. They were at the oversized desk in the outer office this time. Ben didn't want Sydney to see their murder board, the way it had laid out her husband's life in so few marker strokes.

"My sister's come to town to be with me. It really does help, having someone to share the pain with. How's the investigation coming?"

"We've found several new leads and we're following them up now. One of our leads is this song that Caleb was apparently writing. Do you know anything about that?"

Sydney shook her head. "I knew he was working on something, but he wouldn't tell me anything about it until it was finished."

Ben handed her a sheet with the lyrics, which Julie had printed out at the library with much grumbling along the lines of "who doesn't own a printer?"

"Does any of that make sense to you?" Ben asked.

Sydney scanned the sheet. "Sorry, I'm afraid not," she said after a moment. "But we only met after college. He could have written it about something that happened before then, couldn't he?"

"And he never mentioned anything to you? Anything like… Well… I mean this is only a possibility, it might not be what the song was actually about…"

"Yes?"

"At our best guess so far, we think the song might be about rape, or else some other sort of assault. If not Caleb, then someone he knew, maybe?"

Sydney's eyes went wide. "No, he never talked about anything like that. I know he had a good friend who ran away when he was a kid, but other than that, he seemed to have had a nice little childhood."

"That's just a guess, we don't really have much to support it except the lyrics of the song themselves, and that's a soft science at best."

"I understand. I'll let you know if I remember anything, and I can look through some old photographs of Caleb's. I'll let you know if I find anything of note."

"Thanks, Sydney," Ben said, sinking back into the chair, an old wooden thing that creaked ominously under even the lightest strain.

"No, thank you. I really do appreciate the trouble you're going to for me, for us."

Ben smiled and showed Sydney out. No sooner had she stepped out onto the steps than she nearly collided with Julie, who was stomping up them in what Ben thought was the stormiest mood he'd ever anyone in, except perhaps Julie's father after the Incident. In fact, she looked so very like him now that Ben felt a brief thrill of terror. It was the noses, he decided, both of their noses wrinkled up when they were angry. That, and their hazel eyes, which burned from within like they were about to shoot laser beams at anything that had the misfortune to get in their way.

Julie slammed the door open and clomped past Ben into the inner office.

"I'm going to kill Katie next time I see her," she muttered, as she slung her bag around the back of the armchair with more force than what was strictly necessary.

"Please don't," Ben said.

"See, when I had brunch with her a week ago, she threatened to tell everyone I was a stripper—long story—unless I told her what my new job was, and so I told her, and then of course she went and told Trip, because I guess she can't keep a secret to save her life, and then Trip went straight to my parents because I guess it's just too much trouble to stay the hell out of my damn business, and no sooner have I taken a seat before my mother starts begging me to quit, my dad shoots eye daggers at me, and Trip just stares at me with this look of complete pity. Well, I don't need his pity! I don't need anyone's pity! I'm having the time of my fucking life, and they can't seem to realize that for once, just once in my whole damn life, I'd like to actually do what I want to do!" Julie's voice increased in volume as she ranted, until by the end she was screaming and punctuating her sentences with kicks to the legs of the armchair.

"Please be kind to the chair," Ben said. "None of that was its fault."

"Sorry," Julie said, collapsing into said chair. Ben wondered if she was talking to him or to the chair. It was hard to tell with Julie.

"Do they know… I mean, are they aware…"

"They don't know the specific identity of my employer, if that's what you're trying to ask. No, I didn't tell Katie that bit, and it wouldn't have meant anything to her anyway, she doesn't know who you are," Julie said, running a hand through her caramel-colored mane. All of the fight seemed to have drained out of her. When she glanced up at him, it was with a look of complete exhaustion.

"So how mad could they have been?"

Julie shot Ben a look. "Very. I mean, I kind of did the one thing they told me not to do."

There was no hint of accusation in Julie's voice, but all the same Ben felt a pang of guilt. "It comes out of love. You know that, right? They just want you to be safe."

"Aw, hell, I know, but usually that only makes me feel guilty for feeling angry, and then angry all over again because they're using love to justify locking me away from the only thing I actually want to do with my life, and the whole thing starts over again."

"For what it's worth, I'm sorry."

"I know, but really, it's not your fault. I'm happy with the choice I made. I just wish they could be happy for me, too."

"They're not going to, like, disown you or anything over this?"

Julie gave a bitter, humorless chuckle. "No, if anything, they'll try to get closer to me. My dad's fiftieth birthday party is on Friday, now they want me over there early to 'help set up,' which means trying to get me alone so we can 'talk some more.' Some conversation! It's not like they're going to listen to a word I say."

Ben nodded. "What time do you have to be there?"

"Party starts at 5:00, so probably around 3:00. Half an hour drive away, so I'd need to leave at 2:30, 2:00 if I want to get home beforehand."

"How're you getting there? You don't own a car, do you?"

"Trip and I share a car, and he's all over the place for work, so he has dibs. But he's staying at my parents' house for the next few days."

"To help with the party?"

"To get away from me. Wise move. If he didn't, I might start throwing things at him until he did. But he'll be picking me up Friday. Hopefully I'll have calmed down enough by then that I won't try to strangle him on sight."

"Are you going to be okay to talk to Duke tonight?"

"Hmm? Yeah. I'm perfectly fine. Just as long as no one aggravates me."

Ben wasn't particularly reassured, but he didn't want to find out what would happen if he aggravated Julie by saying so, so he kept his mouth shut.

The bar at Rivers was one of those where you felt you could get drunk just off the beer fumes alone. People talked and laughed loudly as they tried to be heard over the buzz of different sports games on the television. Julie counted seven television screens on her first glance around the room, and each tuned to a different sports network. Julie worried, for a second, that their target, a large man with a short black beard and a slightly protruding belly, would be deep in conversation with another patron, but Duke was sitting alone at the wooden bar, his only companion being a very large plate of bacon-topped nachos, which he was wolfing down at an alarming yet, strangely admirable speed. Julie and Ben took the two stools on either side of him. They'd planned this bit in the car on the way there. What Julie hadn't planned for was that the stools would be so high up off the ground that she had to climb it like a small ladder to get on top of it. Once she was settled, she turned to Duke and pretended to have just noticed him.

"OMG!" Julie cried, in a very artificial voice. Ben had a feeling she was enjoying this. "You're that guy on the radio, The Duke!"

Duke looked surprised, but extremely flattered, as Ben had suspected he would be.

"You listen to my show?" he asked, turning away from the basketball game to look at Julie.

"Yeah, whenever me and my BFF Katie are coming back from the club, we tune into your show. But we're at clubs, like, every night, so we listen a lot. I guess you could say I'm kind of a party girl."

Ben cringed as Julie's voice grew more affected and she started twirling her hair around her finger. It occurred to him that this "character" she had adopted would be much more effective had she not been wearing a stained and faded purple sweatshirt from the county fair underneath ragged denim overalls with hand-sewn scrap fabric patches on the knee. Her voice and mannerisms sounded so very fake anyway that he started to doubt it would work at all, unless Duke was either very self-centered or very stupid.

Apparently Duke was at least one of those things, because he sat up a little taller on his squeaky bar stool and flashed Julie a smile he probably thought was charming. "I didn't know I had such dedicated fans."

Julie laughed, a high-pitched girlish giggle that sounded so fake Ben had to bite his lip to keep from laughing. Then she suddenly turned shy. "Can… Can I get a selfie?" she asked, batting her eyelashes, and she pulled her cell phone out from one of the massive pockets in her overalls.

"It'd be my pleasure," Duke said, and he draped one arm over Julie's shoulder and flashed his sleazy smile while Julie snapped the picture.

"Thank you so much, Katie will never believe this!" Julie said, as the phone disappeared into her overalls again. The only thing Ben found harder to believe than Julie's acting was the fact that Duke was actually buying it.

Julie leaned in close. "So, tell me, 'cuz Katie and I are dying to know, who's your Duchess?"

In the dim light of the bar, Ben thought he saw a flicker of discomfort pass over Duke's face, but then it was gone, and Ben wondered if he'd imagined it entirely.

"That's a secret," Duke said, taking another bite from his nachos. A bit of cheese stuck in his beard. He didn't notice.

"Oh, I'm such a sucker for forbidden love!" Julie said.

"What makes you think it's forbidden?"

"Well she's married, isn't she? It's just so tragic, star-crossed lovers, cursed to be apart forever…" Julie said, and she sighed dreamily.

"But you know why I can't tell you, then," Duke said. "I mean, if her husband finds out, then it's all over."

Julie grinned a toothy grin that made her look a bit like a wolf. Or maybe an alligator. "And what a tragedy that would be," she said in her normal voice.

Duke looked very confused. Ben thought it was about time to step in.

"I'm Ben Clydesdale," he said. "I'm investigating the death of Caleb Fredrick."

"Did you kill him?" Julie asked bluntly, still smiling that vaguely predatory smile. Ben glared at her, and for once she took the hint.

"You were in the building when Caleb was stabbed, right?" Ben asked.

Duke seemed to be panicking a little. He made to get up, but Julie rested a hand on his shoulder and forced him back into his seat. "I mean, I guess, but I didn't kill the man!"

"And you didn't hear or see anything?"

"Don't you think I would have told the police already if I had?!"

"Nothing?"

Duke glared at Ben. "No, nothing. I saw Caleb when I came in, he was in the break room, smoking his post-show cigarette, but I didn't stop and talk to him because I was already running late. Normally, that wouldn't be a problem, I have Duchess start the show for me all the time, but she was out that night."

"No cars beside Caleb's in the parking lot?"

Duke laughed nervously. "There were lots of cars beside Caleb's in the parking lot. We share our back lot with Roscoe, and Clarissa's party hadn't quite wrapped up by the time I got there. I don't think she herself left until 1:30. But by 5:00, when I signed off, they were all gone. Just mine, and Caleb's, which wasn't that odd. Sometimes he crashed on the sofa in there, if he was too tired to drive home. The lights had been off in the break-room when I passed by, I'd just assumed he'd turned them off and gone to sleep."

"You didn't linger, after your show was over?"

"No, I went home and got in bed. I have the worst slot, you know. Didn't wake up until afternoon, when some cops showed up on my doorstep asking all those questions. That wasn't odd, either, I mean, me sleeping late, not the cops showing up. My sleep schedule's always like that. It's why Alice left me, the damn time slot. This whole Duke and Duchess thing started as a way to try and make my show more popular, so that I could move to a better slot. I mean, it's just an act, honestly, but still."

"And who is the Duchess?"

"Is that really relevant to your investigation?"

"Potentially," Ben said, trying not to get distracted by Julie, who, out of the corner of his eye, he could see wiggling back and forth impatiently.

"We don't lie about her being married, if her husband found out, it would cause problems."

Julie tried and failed to cock an eyebrow. "I thought you said it was just an act?"

Duke looked back and forth between her and Ben. "No! I mean, yes! It's an act! I mean, but if he found out, he could think it was real!" Little beads of sweat had started to form on Duke's face, and he wiped them away with the back of his hand.

"Frankly, Duke," Julie said, leaning forward. "I don't believe you."

Duke looked like he was about to launch into another passionate denial, but Julie smiled at him again, that horrible toothy smile, and something inside him broke.

"I swear, I'm not in love with her," he said, in a small, defeated voice. "And I don't think she's in love with me, but our relationship isn't strictly limited to the radio either. There's a… physical… element to it as well."

"Did Caleb ever learn who the Duchess was?" Ben asked, ignoring the fact that Julie had just punched the air in triumph. "Or that you two were… involved… outside of the show?"

"No, or if he did, he didn't tell me."

Julie jumped in again. "He didn't ever confront you or her about it? In a hotel room? He didn't tell you that 'the lies had to end'?"

"He did not. If you're talking about the Woodsley trip, I was busy the whole time."

"Let me guess," Julie said. "With your Duchess. The trouble is, Duke, she's the only one who could verify that. And you won't tell us who she is."

"I'm telling the truth, I swear! But I won't tell you who she is, she's got too much to lose."

"I believe you," Ben said, and he did. Duke was sleazy and self-centered, but his watery green eyes were honest. Still, he couldn't muster up much sympathy for the man.

"You do?" Duke asked, looking very relieved. "Thank God."

"Bye, Duke," Julie said, standing up and vaulting down from her stool. "Keep in touch."

Ben followed her, though his legs were long enough that he didn't have to jump. They walked out into the night and toward Ben's car.

"What the hell, Julie?" Ben demanded when they were safely out of earshot. "You could have blown the whole interview!"

"Sorry," Julie said, and she did sound genuine, but she spoke very quickly. "Got carried away, I guess. It won't happen again."

"But?" Ben asked because he sensed a 'but' coming. In the light from the streetlights, he could see that gleam in her eyes, the one she got when she'd thought of something or was about to think of something, and her wolf-like smile had returned in full strength.

"Way back in the beginning, you said Duke was the only person at the station beside Caleb and the killer, right?"

"That's correct. Brittany would have been there, but she was at the gallery opening thing."

Julie's eyes flashed and she grinned wider. Ben stared at her for a second, trying to see how the gears in her mind were turning, because he could tell she had an idea.

"What are you thinking?" he asked.

"Don't you get it?" Julie asked. "Brittany wasn't there that night. Duchess wasn't there that night. And Brittany is married, and from something Cam said, it doesn't sound like a particularly happy marriage."

Ben stared at her. At first, the notion of a stuck-up woman like Brittany bedding a greasy man like Duke seemed preposterous, but the longer he thought about it, the more it made sense.

"Alex said Brittany surprised everyone by coming to the hotel when she didn't normally go to those sorts of things, and her husband wasn't with her. What if she came because Duke would be there?" Ben said slowly.

"I mean, it makes sense, two people stuck in an office in those early hours of the morning, no one else there. Cameron even said that Brittany and Duke were pretty close."

"But how do we verify it?"

"It's pretty easy. 'Hey, Brittany, we know you're fucking Duke Werkle, poor taste, by the way, wanna talk about Caleb now?' "

"Borderline blackmail," Ben pointed out.

"So?"

"So, you might not care, but I do."

"We don't have to threaten to release the information or anything, we just go in and bring it up immediately. She's savvy, she'll realize on her own that while we would never dream of using that information against her, we certainly could."

"Still blackmail. And beside the legal implications, it's just a cruel way to go about doing things. We'll find another way."

CHAPTER 11:
Murder with Tea

On Wednesday morning, by some coincidence, Ben and Julie arrived at the office at the exact same time.

"I have some other ways we could get Brittany to talk," Julie said, as Ben parked his car and got out. After weeks of sleet and icy winds, it was a surprisingly pleasant day. Spring proper wouldn't come for another month or two, but Ben was enjoying this brief taste.

"What?" Ben asked, wary of what Julie's 'other ways' would entail, given that her first thought had been blackmail. But the words that came out of her mouth next were surprisingly sensible.

"Call up Lianna, see if she'd be willing to set up a meeting between us and her and Brittany. Well, probably just you would be better, since Lianna already knows you, and doesn't know me. But that's not important, whatever the case, with Lianna there, Brittany won't be able to run out as easily, and Lianna should be able to keep her from taking a go at you. And when you talk, open with the fact that it was Sydney who hired you, that she came to you, not the other way around, that should put her fears that you're preying on grief and tragedy or whatever at rest."

"I wish I'd thought of that," Ben said, as he unlocked the door and they stepped inside.

"Beats blackmail, anyway," Julie muttered, but she seemed pleased.

Lianna seemed genuinely thrilled by the idea when Ben called to ask her.

"Absolutely. It's about time she learned to keep an open mind about people, even if she doesn't end up having anything substantial to contribute to your investigation."

"What time works best?"

"I can get her over here as early as this afternoon, if that suits you. Tell me, Mr. Clydesdale, do you like tea?"

"Tea?" Ben asked, wondering if he'd heard correctly.

"Yes, I think an afternoon tea will set the mood quite nicely. It'll add an air of decorum that I think will help keep things civil. I'll see you at 3:00, then."

They said goodbye and Ben hung up.

"We're having afternoon tea with the Burbans," he told Julie.

"We? I'm coming with you?"

"I think so. I want you to be there at least to watch, but maybe don't talk unless someone asks you a direct question."

"What, you don't trust me?"

Ben gave Julie a look. She sighed.

"I get it. I wouldn't trust me, either."

They arrived at Lianna's door at 2:55. The house was very grand, made of red-brown stone and covered in ivy. The ivy was brown and shriveled now, but Ben imagined that in the summer it would be beautiful. It wasn't quite as large as he'd expected, but he had a feeling that was less a representation of limited funds and more a deliberate choice in favor of manageability.

Lianna let them in herself. "Come in. Everything's set up in the sitting room."

"Is Brittany here yet?" Ben asked.

"No. Is this your assistant? You mentioned her on the phone."

"Yes, this is Julie Bernard," Ben said.

"Bernard… Are you a relation of Trip Bernard?"

Julie nodded. "Yes ma'am, he's my brother."

"Lovely young man. Good musician, too, and his art is fantastic. Watercolors and sketches, some charcoal, right?"

"Yes ma'am."

"Well, sit down, make yourselves comfortable," Lianna said, when they came to the little sitting room.

Everything in the living room was pastel-colored, the rug, the curtains, the furniture, even the artwork, which was interspersed in between black-and-white photographs of people Ben assumed were members of Lianna's family, past and present. The whole place smelled of dried flowers and peppermint.

Julie sat down in one of two quilted armchairs, Ben on a dandelion-yellow couch. On the coffee table between them was a tea tray and several plates of little cakes and cookies. Julie glanced at them hungrily.

The doorbell rang again, and Lianna went off to answer it. Ben stood up and straightened his suit jacket and tie. Lianna returned, and Brittany came in behind her.

"What are you doing here?" Brittany demanded when she saw them.

Ben decided to follow Julie's advice. "I was hired by Sydney Fredrick to investigate Caleb's death," he said immediately. It seemed to work well enough.

"I see," Brittany said, icy but no longer aggressive, and she took a seat on the green chaise lounge. Ben sat back down, and Lianna took the chair next to Julie. Lianna and Julie poured tea for everyone. Neither Ben nor Brittany made any moves toward their cups.

"What about her?" Brittany asked, jerking her head at Julie, who had now taken a lemon cookie from the tray and was dunking it in her tea. "She's a reporter, isn't she?"

"Not anymore," Ben said. "She quit, she works with me now."

"Huh," was the only reply, which Ben had no idea how to take. He plunged on anyway.

"Ms. Burban, what's your relationship to Duke Werkle?"

Brittany's eyes went wide and she tensed on the edge of her seat, as if getting ready to flee. "Duke? He works at the station, I suppose that would make us colleagues."

Ben decided a small lie was probably fine. "Duke told us the identity of his Duchess yesterday. And that your relationship extended beyond his show."

Brittany glared at him but settled back down into the couch. "It was never anything romantic, you understand. Those late nights, well, early mornings, I guess, they're awfully boring. We got to talking during Duke's commercial breaks. It all went from there."

Out of the corner of his eyes, Ben saw Julie give him a little self-satisfied smirk before downing another cookie. "Did Caleb ever confront you about it? At the hotel trip you all took, maybe?"

"I wasn't under the impression that he was even aware. If he did, he kept quiet about it. Caleb was good like that, he was good at keeping secrets."

"Was he now?"

"He was the quiet sort. He saw a lot, but he didn't talk much, only when he had something valuable to say. And he wasn't a gossip. A lot of the others at the station are. Maybe the job attracts them, I don't know."

"It sounded like reporters have been a frequent concern at the station, this last month."

Brittany sniffed. "Vultures, the lot of them. We've a business to run, and we're dealing with our own grief on top of it. Don't know what they think they're doing," she said, and then she pivoted and turned to Julie, who was happily sipping tea with Lianna. "You. You were at the station on Monday, talking to Clarissa Byron. What for?"

"To see if she knew anything relevant to Caleb's death," Julie said, taking a small cake from the tray and downing it in one bite.

"Hmph."

"That's the truth," Ben said. "One last thing. Did you see anyone suspicious, around the radio station ever? Or at the hotel?"

"The Woodsley trip? I'm afraid I wasn't really in a mood to notice anything there. I'd come in on a flight from LA the night before, and somewhere along the line, my luggage was lost. I ended up buying a lot of replacement things there, at the hotel boutique. I was a bit too preoccupied with my own troubles to notice anything out of the ordinary."

Ben felt his phone vibrate in his pocket, but he ignored it. "And at the radio station? In the weeks leading up to Caleb's death?"

"Nothing."

"Well, thank you anyway," Ben said, and he stood up. "Julie?"

Julie gulped down the remains of her tea and grabbed one last cookie from the tray.

"Thanks, I've had a lovely time," she said to Lianna, and then she followed Ben out the door.

When they were back in the car, Ben checked his phone to see who had tried to call him. He was expecting perhaps Lila checking in, or maybe his mother. Maybe it would even be Julie's father, having somehow figured out that she was working for him. Ben shivered at the thought.

But it was none of those people. At first, when he saw the number, Ben had no idea who it was, and then he remembered. Alex Harcourt.

"Alex tried to call me," Ben told Julie.

"Well call her back! Maybe she's found something!"

Ben called Alex. She picked up after the second ring.

"Mr. Clydesdale? I just remembered something. I think I told the police at the time, but I forgot afterward."

"What is it?"

"The blue hoodie that the person Caleb was arguing with wasn't plain, it had a logo on it."

"What did the logo look like?"

"Three trees, the ones on the outside were taller and sort of out at an angle, and the one in the middle was shorter and straight. And their branches were bare, no leaves. The whole thing was in silver. Does that make any sense?"

"Enough. Thanks, Alex, this could be huge," and Ben hung up.

"What is it?" Julie asked eagerly.

"The guy who was arguing with Caleb was wearing a sweatshirt with a logo on it."

Julie whipped out a notebook and a pen. "Describe it."

"Alex said it showed three trees in a row. The two on the outside were taller and went out at an angle, the one in the middle was shorter and straight up-and-down. All of their branches were bare, like winter. This was all in silver, on a blue backdrop, in case the colors are important," Ben relayed. Julie made a quick sketch and held it out to show Ben.

"Like this?"

"I guess, you'd have to ask Alex."

"Take a photo and text it to her," Julie suggested. Ben did so and waited as the dot-dot-dot response bubble appeared. Then: "Yeah. Like that."

"Alex said that's it," Ben reported. "You can start looking for that when we get back."

CHAPTER 12:
Dead Ends

Julie's search was still unfruitful by the time Ben judged she ought to go home and get some sleep.

"It's not Roscoe, it's not the Woodsley, it's not Rivers, it's not the Palatine. It's definitely not the radio station, their logo is very early 2000s, and it's not any of the other local radio stations, either. It's not a restaurant. It's not a major hotel chain, and it's not one of the dwindling number of independent bookstores. Given our clientele, I also checked all the record shops, and I'll move on to recording studios tomorrow," Julie said, rubbing her forehead.

"Go home," Ben ordered. "We can pick this back up tomorrow."

"Yeah," Julie said. It was a sure sign of her exhaustion that she didn't even protest. She just stuffed the list of crossed-out businesses into her bag and slung it over her shoulder.

"Want a ride?" Ben offered, realizing that it was pitch black out.

"That'd be great."

For once, Ben realized, it didn't feel right to talk about the case. Then he realized that they didn't have anything to talk about beside the case, unless he counted the tension between Julie's job and her family, which he didn't think either of them really wanted to talk about.

"How's Lila?" Julie asked, after a minute's uncomfortable silence passed.

"She's good," Ben said.

"You've been married, what, twenty-five years now?"

"Sounds about right, we got married pretty young, right out of college. Actually, she was still in college."

Julie nodded. "My parents married right out of college, too," she said, though Ben already knew this.

"Yep. Your dad and I, we actually went to the same school, though he was a few years ahead of me."

"Yep."

Another minute of awkward silence.

"I'll put the radio on," Ben offered, and suddenly the silence was banished by Beethoven. Very, very loud Beethoven. Julie clapped her hands over her ears. Ben shouted something that might have been a curse, but it was unintelligible over the blast, and cranked the volume way down.

"Sorry 'bout that," he said, when their ears had recovered.

"All good," Julie said.

"Sometimes when my radio turns off, the volume resets to full," Ben explained.

"I get it. On our car, the date automatically resets to 4:00 AM, January 1, 2002. Every time you turn the car off and on. The damn thing didn't even exist in 2002."

"Maybe it's a time machine."

Julie laughed. "Maybe."

They were in front of her apartment now.

"I'll see you tomorrow," Julie said, as she got out of the car.

"Tomorrow."

Tomorrow dawned, and Julie woke feeling very well rested, and though she had no ideas that would help her identify Alex's logo, she was determined to attack the day with renewed energy and vigor. At least, that was how she phrased it during a morning self-pep-talk as she brushed her teeth and worked her tangled mane back into neat twin braids.

In order to prove her renewed energy and vigor, both to herself and to the universe as a whole, she decided to stop by her favorite coffee shop on the way to work. She ordered a large black coffee and picked a donut from the glass case at the counter. She wolfed down the donut (chocolate icing and sprinkles) and drank the coffee as she walked. It had turned cold again, after the brief respite, but the heat of the coffee kept away the worst of it, like a talisman protecting against evil.

She was passing the local library when she finished the coffee and jogged the few steps between her and the nearest trash bin, which was right in front of the library doors.

The Closefield Springs Public Library was a rather magnificent building, more like a courthouse or a house of legislature than a public library. Hurriedly, Julie picked up her phone and texted Ben to let him know she'd be late.

Even at this early hour, there were a handful of people milling about. A very goth-looking teenager who was probably intending to skip school was lurking by the manga in the back corner. A woman not much older than Julie in a brightly colored patchwork dress was setting up some sort of activity in the children's corner. An older man was typing frantically at one of the computers in the middle of the room. Two librarians sat behind the very high desk just ahead.

Julie went up to them. The younger (but by no means young) of the two, a woman in her mid-fifties with short graying curls and a pair of very round Harry-Potter-style glasses perched low on her nose looked up—or rather, down—at her.

"Can I help you?" she asked. Her name tag read "Edith." Of course she would be an Edith.

"Do you know anything about this?" Julie asked, showing Edith the drawing she'd made of the logo as Ben had described it.

"No, love, sorry."

"It's fine, thanks anyway," Julie said. It had been worth a shot, if the logo was something from a fictional series. Of course, if that were the case, it would be much harder to find out who would have been wearing it. Julie imagined scouring through online fan chat rooms, and shuddered at the thought.

She was about to leave when she saw a shelf marked "Yearbooks." She went over to it on a whim. All of them were from Closefield Elementary, Closefield Middle, and Riverview High, the local public schools in the area, which she and Trip—and Caleb, Cameron, Luke, and Danny—had attended. She found the 2001-2002 book for Closefield Middle, and started flipping through it. Danny's picture jumped out at her immediately from the ranks of awkward pre-teens. It was the same photo that had been used for the missing posters.

Julie snapped the book shut and carried it over to the desk.

"Can I check this out?"

Edith sounded surprised. Julie figured the yearbooks probably didn't get checked out that often. "I suppose."

Julie handed Edith the book and dug her library card from her wallet. Edith scanned the card and stamped the book, then handed both back to Julie, who tucked them into her bag

"Have a nice day!" Julie called over her shoulder, and she walked away.

"And you thought this would be important why?" Ben asked when Julie showed him the book.

"It's just more information about them as kids, isn't it?" Julie said. The color in the pictures was faded, and some of the pages had torn corners. Julie closed it and examined the cover. It showed neon pink and green triangles over a black background, and the words in white: "A Year to Remember."

"Looks pretty 80s for the turn of the century," Ben said with a raised eyebrow. Julie shrugged and stuffed the book into her bag to examine at her leisure.

"Retro is considered cool, you know."

"If you say so."

"Hey man, your whole vibe is retro. The suits, this office, those glasses…"

Ben pretended to be hurt. "I like my glasses."

Julie laughed and pulled out her computer to cross more things off of her growing list.

"It's not the Closefield Recording Studio," she said after a while, running a line through that item.

Twenty minutes later: "It's not any of the annual recurring music events."

One hour later: "It's not from a major music or art event in the last ten years."

Two hours later, she gave up.

"This is ridiculous!" she said, closing her laptop. Ben looked up from his desk, where he was organizing the case folders.

"Still nothing?" he asked, but he knew the answer.

"Okay, let's think. The person is probably someone we've already looked at, so someone involved in either the radio station itself, or the local music scene as a whole. If the sweatshirt is from an event, it's more likely to be something musical. Not most likely, more likely."

"Try looking closely at the logo instead. A lot of logos show letters."

Julie squinted at her sketch. "It could be a W, I guess. Or an M. If it were turned 90 degrees, it could be an E as well. Or a three."

"So look at businesses and events that start with any of those letters. Or prominently feature the number three. And maybe things that have something to do with trees or nature."

With renewed vigor, Julie opened up her laptop and started typing, but thirty minutes later, she looked just as defeated as she had before. "It's not from an environmental event," she said dejectedly. "Most of their logos show the earth some way or another. There was one called 'World-savers' that I thought might be it, but its logo is a sort of superman type dude with the earth on its chest instead of the superman logo. And in blue and green instead of blue and red."

"Maybe it's some sort of music in the park or outdoor art show?" Ben suggested. Julie typed again, and again deflated like a sad balloon.

"There's only one of those, it's called Music in the Park, so again, promising, but the logo is a kind of overgrown guitar, all covered in vines and stuff."

Ben thought for a moment. "Have you checked the Woodsley yet?"

"Yes, it's some stupid golf thing."

"Right."

Eventually, Julie decided the more efficient way would be to scan suspects' social media accounts for sightings of the hoodie. If nothing else, it would give her search engine a bit of a break.

She checked Alex Harcourt's Instagram first, and for a second, she thought she'd found it, in the first picture, Alex was wearing a blue sweatshirt. But then, why would Alex have told them about the hoodie in the first place? Or the argument at all? And indeed, when Julie looked closer, she saw that Alex's hoodie had a different logo, one Julie recognized with her new logo expertise as Closefield Recording Studios. It showed a microphone with a smiley face, and it was printed in tie-die colors instead of silver. She checked the other pictures on Alex's page, but no other blue hoodies appeared.

She checked Caleb's page next, figuring that all of the people closest to him would appear at some point or another, but Caleb's social media remained as unforthcoming as it had been when she'd first started looking at it, so many weeks previously. Caleb hadn't been very active online, which didn't exactly surprise Julie, but it was quite frustrating. His last post had been over a month before he died, and that had been a picture of him and Sydney at a swanky restaurant. No blue hoodies, no hoodies of any kind, only sport coats and fancy dresses. Even as she scrolled back, she couldn't find any photos of the radio staff at all, except for Alex, but even she only appeared in a few. It was mostly just Caleb and Sydney, and one or two pictures of an older woman with Caleb's nose and big dark-brown eyes, who Julie assumed was Caleb's mother.

Julie realized she'd been staring off into space, and shook herself. It was nearly lunchtime, anyway, but Julie wasn't hungry.

"I'm going to take a walk," she said. "Clear my head."

Ben nodded. "Go. Come back when you're ready, not before."

"Right," Julie said, and she pulled on her coat and hat. The hat was a fluffy pink thing with a giant hot-pink pompom on the top. It was more than a little too big for her, so that it came down just past her eyebrows.

"Katie went through a knitting phase last year," Julie explained when she saw Ben staring at her with a badly suppressed grin. "It's very warm."

"It looks it," Ben said, trying his best to keep a straight face, but it was difficult. The hat made Julie look even younger than she was, almost childish.

"Whatever," Julie said, and she was out the door.

She walked twice around the block and decided that was probably long enough. She'd done the same thing in high school and college, during exam seasons. It didn't matter if it was a short walk, or a bike ride, or a run. Or maybe a few rounds of Mario-Kart, if she was feeling lazy. Something, anything, to give her mind a break.

But today she'd left her bike at home, and she no longer owned a video game console, and she didn't have running shoes with her. But walking around wasn't giving her much of a rest, because the hat had got her thinking about Katie, and the fact that they hadn't made up with each other yet.

Julie had met Katie at college; they were roommates freshman year, and they had been close friends ever since. Katie had other friends, Matti, her current roommate, for one, but Julie didn't. They had fought once or twice over the years, but never very hard or for very long, and Julie was starting to miss her, as exasperating as she could be sometimes.

But, Julie told herself, she wasn't the one who needed to apologize. Maybe she'd overreacted, but it had been Katie who had made the first comments, Katie who had tattled on her to Trip. No, Julie wasn't going to apologize before Katie did, no matter how long it took.

When she came back to Ben's green door the second time, she decided that even trawling through information without a result would be better than being alone with her thoughts, so she climbed up the stone steps, and almost slipped in the ice that coated the top step. When it had gotten warmer, the snow had melted, but overnight it had frozen again, creating little death traps if you weren't watching where you were going, which Julie was not. She flailed, caught the wrought iron railing, and steadied herself. Then, carefully this time, she opened the door and stepped inside.

Ben looked up when Julie came back in and shed her bulky black coat and fluffy pink hat.

"Refreshed?" he asked.

"Yep, definitely," Julie lied.

She sat back down in her armchair and pulled out her laptop again. The battery was dead. No problem, she carried a spare charger in her bag. Except she'd loaned it to Trip the week before, and he'd left before she had a chance to get it back.

Julie sighed. "Got a charger?"

Ben tossed her his and she plugged her computer in at the outlet near the filing cabinets. Then she sat down again and opened up the yearbook, because she had nothing else to do.

"Did you know Danny and Cameron were in the school broadcasting club?" Julie asked.

"I did not," Ben said.

Julie flipped a few pages and found a photo of a young Caleb holding up a trophy shaped like a king from a chess board. "Caleb was in chess club, apparently he won an in-school tournament."

In the back of the book, there was a whole page dedicated to Danny. Different students had written notes to him, and the school had printed them around a photograph of Danny, a better one than his slightly fuzzy school picture. "Danny, if you're reading this, we miss you and we want you to come back," and "Danny, the broadcasting club wants its Vice President back." There were no notes from Caleb or Cameron, or if there were, then they were unsigned. Julie wondered why that was. Maybe his friends thought the whole thing was pointless and trite. That's what Julie thought, at least.

By now, her computer was charged enough that Julie could use it, though she had to move from her nice comfy chair to sit on the floor where the charging cord could reach. Julie had no excuse to continue flipping through the yearbook, so she had to go back to scanning social media pages.

When it got time to leave, Julie still had nothing, and was on the verge of tearing her hair out.

"I don't get it!" she said, as she packed up for the day. "No one has any photos with the blue sweatshirt. No businesses or events have the three trees as their logo! It's like it doesn't exist!"

"We can keep looking tomorrow," Ben said, though he had a feeling it wasn't helping, a feeling which was confirmed by the withering glare Julie shot him.

"What if Alex was lying about the whole thing? What if we're on a wild goose chase?"

"You think she killed Caleb?"

"Maybe they got in a fight about the song? She wanted more credit than he was going to give her? And she lied about the blue hoodie and overhearing the argument to deflect suspicion, if someone did overhear it."

Ben took off his glasses and started rubbing the lenses clean with his shirt. "It's possible, I suppose. I really hope it's not Alex, though, I liked her, she seemed like a nice kid."

Julie sighed. "I don't really think it's her either. I'm just mad at her for this stupid lead which doesn't seem to go anywhere."

Ben sighed. "It's okay. Maybe tomorrow we can find a different angle beside the logo."

Julie nodded wearily, stuffed her ridiculous pink hat onto her head, and left before Ben could offer to give her another ride home.

CHAPTER 13:
Glimpses

Julie did not feel a renewed burst of energy the next morning. It didn't help that she found her bag of coffee empty and the bananas in the bowl on her kitchen counter had turned black and greasy. And it really didn't help that she had several hours alone with her family to look forward to that afternoon.

The wind had picked up as well, so that her walk to Ben's office was little short of miserable, and her stupid too-big hat was blown clear off her head and landed in a dirty puddle. She picked it up and twisted it to get most of the water out, but it was still too wet to put in her bag, so she had to carry it the rest of the way, the cold gray water slowly soaking through her glove.

In Ben's outer office, she draped the hat and her wet glove over the arm of the sofa to dry and went into the inner office.

"Where's your other glove?" Ben asked when she came in.

"Drying."

Ben decided not to ask any further questions, Julie didn't look like she was in the mood for it.

"Let's work on something else beside the logo today," he suggested.

That seemed to lighten Julie's mood. "What, then?"

Ben grinned. "I got video. From a security camera."

Julie sat up and her eyes grew bright. "I thought there wasn't any footage from the radio station?" she asked.

"There isn't, but there is a camera behind Roscoe's. So I called their manager, who put me in touch with their security. That's when I met Edward, who might just be my new best friend. You see, normally the cameras only actually store up to forty-eight hours, but when Caleb was killed, he saved the footage from that night, in case it became important. And when I asked, very politely, by the way, he sent it over to me."

Julie leaped from her chair and came around to behind Ben's desk. "Let's see it."

Ben pulled up the footage and turned up the speed. It was from an angle where the door to the radio station and most of the parking lot was visible. Julie could just see the dumpster, behind which was the back door to the restaurant, and a small sliver of the street beyond was just in view, where cars and people passed by at accelerated velocities. It grew dark, and the streetlights flicked on, casting strange shadows in the parking lot.

A car appeared, and a figure sped into the radio station. "There's Caleb going in," Ben said, and a few minutes later, they saw Clarissa Byron, in a fancy long red coat, and a neat and elaborate hairdo, coming out and heading out on foot to the street and presumably toward the front door of the restaurant.

A long time passed, and Ben clicked up the speed a few notches. He saw the flash of Duke's car arriving at 12:09, and he turned the speed down a few notches.

Duke got out and walked into the radio station.

"Come on now," Julie whispered.

At 12:56, a dark figure appeared from behind the dumpster, though whether they'd come from the street, or the restaurant, or perhaps had been lurking there all day, Julie couldn't tell. Ben immediately paused, rewound, and slowed down the footage. The figure reemerged, their face hidden in shadow by the hood of their parka. They looked around briefly, then ran into the radio station. Fifteen minutes later, they reappeared and darted back the way they came.

"Can you freeze on them?" Julie asked. Ben rewound and did so, but their mystery person—Caleb's killer—remained unidentifiable. The bulk of the coat could have hidden any body shape, and the hood kept the face in shadow.

"This is bullcrap!" Julie shouted, kicking the leg of the desk. "We're so close! The killer is right freakin' there! And yet we don't have any more idea who it is than we did at the beginning!"

"It's something to confront people with," Ben suggested. "We could go around, show it to the suspects, see how they react?"

"And who would we show it to first?" Julie asked, going back to her own chair and sagging into it.

"Who do we think, out of all the people we've interviewed, had the most reason and the best chance to kill Caleb?" Ben asked.

"Brittany Burban and Duke Werkle," Julie said immediately. "They've got their alibis, but they could have slipped out long enough from their respective places to kill him. That's if Caleb knew about their affair, and we don't know that he did."

"Duke was in the station already, that can't be him," Ben said, pointing to the figure on his screen.

"They could have met at the station, and killed him together," Julie suggested.

"It would have been hard for them to sync up their schedules, though," Ben pointed out. "Both of them had such narrow windows of opportunity."

"What about Alex? The blue hoodie thing is really starting to look like a wild goose chase."

"It's possible. But she has an alibi, too. Not just her parents, but her parents' friends were able to vouch that she was at dinner, and then the movies."

"It went that late?" Julie asked.

"Midnight premiere."

"Great. And there's no chance she could have slipped out of the theater and come back?"

"The movie theater is on the other side of town, it's a decent drive. Would have taken her at least forty-five minutes round trip, if you factored in the time it would take to go in, find Caleb, and kill him."

"So she'd probably have been missed," Julie said, biting her lip.

"What about Luke Sebastian?"

"What would his motive have been, though?" Julie asked.

Ben shrugged. "Jealousy, maybe? He didn't want his friend to release a song, edge in on his territory?"

Julie shook her head. "Luke's not like that."

"Are you sure? You only barely know him."

Julie's voice grew more tense. "We bonded over childhood traumas, I know him well enough."

Ben didn't particularly want to argue, not with Julie in the mood she was in, so he didn't respond.

"I'm going out to buy something for lunch," he said. "We need something fun today."

"Great," Julie said.

Ben couldn't get out fast enough.

When he came back, Julie was looking much calmer, and sat lazily flipping through the old yearbook in her chair.

"Anything interesting?" Ben asked, as he set the soup and sandwiches he'd bought down on the table. Chicken noodle and grilled cheese. And two bottles of sparkling lemonade to go with it.

"Not really," Julie said, as she stood up and came over to investigate the food. She picked up one of the sandwiches and unwrapped the waxed paper, then took a tentative bite.

"Nice," she said, around a mouthful of toasted bread and melted cheese.

Ben handed her one of the paper cups of soup. She took it gratefully and went back to her chair, where she sat with the soup perched between her knees and the sandwich in one hand.

"Sorry," Julie said, thankfully after swallowing this time. "Bad mood, today. This stupid party…"

"Look," Ben said. "Your family is important. More important than this job. But if you're really sure about your choice, then why are you afraid to be confronted with it?"

Julie froze, her sandwich halfway to her lips. She lowered her sandwich. "I don't know that I am. Afraid, I mean."

"What's the worst that could happen?" Ben asked.

"My dad could order me to quit, I guess. Or he could go after you, make you fire me."

"Richard's a good man, Julie, I don't think he'd do that."

"But it's not like I'm uncertain of my choices, honestly."

Ben decided not to press the issue.

Julie resumed looking at the old yearbook as she finished her lunch.

"It really is very retro," she said, examining the cover again.

Ben looked up. "I didn't think of that."

"Think of what?"

"Businesses reprinting old logos onto new merchandise. For the sentimental value."

Julie sat up, throwing chicken noodle soup across the room. "Ah, crap, sorry," she said, and she wiped chicken off her lap. "But that's brilliant!"

"You would have been too young to remember, if you were even around, but about twenty years ago, there was a huge controversy because the Woodsley changed its logo to go with something that emphasized their golf courses after they added the new putting green."

Julie grabbed her laptop from her bag, which had thankfully been spared the chicken noodle shower, and started typing frantically. Then she stopped, clicked once, and grinned.

"Retro Woodsley Sweatshirt with Hood, old Woodsley logo in silver on back, comes in both green and blue. Available exclusively at the hotel boutique!"

Julie looked up at Ben. They stared at each other for a moment, and then, almost simultaneously, cried "Brittany Burban!"

"But…" Julie said, looking up at the clock. It was 2:00, and she had to change into non-soup-soaked clothing before she left for the party.

"Go. Your family is more important."

Julie nodded regretfully, then stuffed her laptop back into her bag, shoved on her coat, and slung her bag onto her shoulder. She ran out, almost forgot her hat and glove, turned back, grabbed them from the arm of the sofa (where they left two damp spots behind) and flew through the door and down the steps.

CHAPTER 14:
Answered Questions, Questioning Answers

Trip picked Julie up from their apartment at 2:30. He got out of the car and stared at her for a moment, then gave her an awkward hug.

"Hey," he said, in a very stiff voice.

"Hello," Julie said, her voice matching his, stiffness for stiffness, ice for ice.

They sat in awkward silence as Trip navigated through town. He turned on the radio eventually, blaring bad country music. Julie missed Ben's Beethoven. She would have preferred a dozen full-volume Beethoven symphonies over a single lab-brewed fake-banjo country song.

Finally, after what seemed like eons but was really only thirty minutes, they pulled up in front of Julie's parents' house.

It was a neat little house. The outside was all a light shade of shale gray with white trimmings. There was a little stone porch outside the front door, where two rocking chairs had sat for as long as Julie could remember. Low flowering bushes ran up against the house. In the spring and summer, they would be gorgeous, with fat white petals and bright green leaves, but now they were scrawny and winter-brown.

It was their mother who greeted them at the door. Theresa Bernard was a large woman, nearly six feet tall, with curly brown hair which was only just starting to gray. She wore it tied back in a ponytail, keeping it clear of her friendly round face.

"Julie! You're here!" she said, sounding a bit surprised, but genuinely pleased that Julie had come, even come early as she'd been asked.

"Of course I'm here," Julie said, and after a moment, Theresa beamed and gave her daughter a hug that smelled of nutmeg and cinnamon.

Julie followed her mother into the narrow dimly-lit hall and hung her coat up on the hook. When she was seven, her father had bought little ladybug hooks and mounted them all around the house. Even now, they made Julie smile.

They walked through the wide archway into the kitchen. It was a small brightly-lit low-ceilinged room at the back of the house, with a gleaming white tile floor and bluebird wallpaper. The furnishings, all of which had shiny silver fixtures, took up most of the space and left little room for people. On the marble counter, various baked goods had been arrayed in a display that most professional bakeries couldn't have hoped to best. There was a massive carrot cake, a favorite of Julie's father, and two berry pies, and several dozen chocolate cupcakes with perfect swirls of icing and rainbow sprinkles.

"The caterer should be here any minute, Trip, can you keep a lookout? Julie, you can help me with the decorations."

"Right," Julie said, setting the small wrapped present she'd brought on the table with the others. Already a small mountain was forming, of gifts that those who would be absent had sent. Julie's had been wrapped hurriedly using newspaper and yarn. It looked very out of place in the sea of perfect cornered, brightly colored, ornately ribboned others, like an ostrich that had wandered into a pride of peacocks. She hoped, at least, that the contents, an ebony fountain pen she'd purchased at a little bookstore not far from her apartment, would suffice.

Theresa handed Julie a string of large blue and white paper tassel things and a roll of tape. "Hang that up over the entryway and then come back."

Julie felt like she was a teenager again. "Go put your laundry away and then come back. Go take out the trash and then come back." She had to get a stepladder to do it, but she managed to get the tassels hung neatly. Then she went back.

The caterer had arrived, and Trip and Theresa were carrying large aluminum trays of food in and setting them up in the kitchen.

Theresa checked her watch. "Oh, Trip, don't you have to pick Annie up from the airport? If you want to be back before the party starts, you need to leave now."

"Right. Thanks, Mom. I'll be back soon," Trip said, setting down the last of his trays and running out.

There was a moment's pause as Theresa pretended be engrossed by the task of lining the trays up perfectly. Julie stood behind the counter, waiting for whatever would come next. Theresa straightened a covered foil tray. Julie knew what her mother was going to say. She didn't want to deal with this right now, she couldn't deal with this right now. She felt her heart beating faster, harder, she wanted to run, and hide, and not come out until her parents were suitably distracted. But instead she stood there, examining the grimy laces of her black converse high-tops, trying to keep her face tight and calm, under control. That was hard. Julie didn't want to stay under control. She wanted to scream and run away, or, even better, teleport far, far away. Maybe a mountaintop cabin in the middle of nowhere, or a houseboat in the middle of a big deep lake. No. Control. She had to keep control. She wouldn't yell, she wouldn't fight, she'd be calm, and she'd listen, and she'd explain in a measured and sane voice.

The blow she was waiting for was about to come when Theresa turned to face her, and with a stiff attempt at casual-ness, removed her apron and wiped her hands clean on a paper towel

"So, dear," Theresa said, in the sort of tense and artificial voice that shows that the person using it was trying to sound casual and conversational.

"Yes, Mom?"

"This job you've taken, are you really sure it's what you want to do?"

"Yes, I'm sure."

"But what if you get hurt again, sweetie?"

"People get hurt every day, regardless of whether they're cops or private detectives. Car accidents, bar fights, murders in a radio station…" Julie realized her mistake too late. She had always been flippant about the things that were bothering her. The therapists she'd seen after the Incident had said that she used humor as a coping mechanism. But to her mother, she supposed it sounded a bit callous. Worse, it revealed that not only was she working at a private detective agency, but she was investigating a murder.

Her mother's gaze turned sharp. "You're not looking into that, are you? The Caleb Fredrick murder?"

"No, Mom," Julie lied, hoping her face remained impassive, hoping she'd gotten better at lying over the last few years, or that her mother had lost the super-human lie detection abilities she'd shown when Julie was younger. It had always been Julie's lies that she'd spotted, and not Trip's, either. "I've just been following it on the news, is all."

Theresa's suspicions were not put completely to rest. "Hmph," was all she said, but she packed a great deal of nuance into the monosyllable.

"Look, my point is, life happens, and sometimes life means getting hurt. And—And what use is it, to have me not doing the things I want to do, the things I love to do, if I could get hit by a bus tomorrow anyway?"

Julie's mother did not seem entirely satisfied, but to Julie's great relief, she let the topic drop for the moment, and sent Julie off with more tassel strings to hang, banners to tie to rusty nails that had been stuck in the walls as long as Julie could remember, and streamers to drape all over the place, until the whole first floor of the house looked very festive and very much like a fire hazard.

Julie's father came through the door then, carrying a paper bag of various glass liquor bottles.

"Go help your dad unload the car," Julie's mother suggested/ordered, and Julie jogged outside, hugging herself to keep warm because she'd left her coat inside, and grabbed a couple of boxes of soda from the open trunk of Richard's car. Then she executed a complex elbow-and-knee maneuver to close the truck without dropping the soda.

She carried the boxes back inside and sat them down with a thud-clang onto one of the stools in the kitchen and turned around to face Round Two: grown daughter versus both parents together. It didn't seem like a fair matchup to Julie.

"Ah! Julie! Look, I wondered if we could talk for a minute—" her father began.

"I already tried, Rick, she wouldn't budge," Theresa called from the living room, where she was setting up the drinks table. "Julie, could you bring those sodas in here, love?"

Julie picked up the boxes again and carried them in to the living room, her father trailing behind her.

"Look, it's just that we care about you, Jules, we don't want to see you getting hurt again," he said.

"She has a counter for that," Theresa said dryly. "It involves getting hit by a bus."

And so on for the next hour and a half.

When Trip's car pulled up in the driveway, Julie wanted to run out and greet him, but she was stuck laying out red and white checkered plastic tablecloths over the folding table her mother had erected in the middle of the kitchen, so she had to content herself with craning her head to watch through the kitchen window. Trip and Annie seemed to be moving at a slow-motion pace just to irritate her. Finally, finally she heard the sound of footsteps on the porch and the creak of the door opening, and then voices in the hall. Trip and Annie emerged into the kitchen, carrying between themselves Annie's two suitcases, her tote bag, and her purse.

"Finally!" Julie muttered.

"Hi, Julie," Annie said, gracious as ever. Even after just getting off a plane, Annie looked neat and put-together. Her dark hair shimmered in the light like ripples in a pond.

"Hi Annie," Julie said, shaking Annie's hand. She wondered what Trip had told Annie in the car. "Be nice to my sister, she's going through a rough patch. Quit her job, out of the blue, and started poking into people's lives for a living."

Theresa poked her head through the doorway. "Come on in!" she said to Trip and Annie, who both hung up their coats and came through into the kitchen.

Jazz played quietly over the old Bluetooth speaker Richard had bought nearly five years ago. Both the kitchen and the living room beyond had been hung with decorations, making the house feel like some sort of festival ground.

Julie's parents had both changed into party clothes, stylish and nice but thankfully not overly formal. Julie looked only a little slovenly in comparison.

The doorbell rang, and Julie went to open it.

It was Rosie Robinson.

"Julie?! Look at you, you're all grown up!" she said, dragging Julie into a hug.

"Nice to see you, Rosie," Julie said, her voice muffled against Rosie's floral print coat.

"Rosie!" This was Richard, standing in the doorway.

Rosie released Julie and turned to Richard.

"Happy Birthday, Rick," she said, handing him her gift. Rosie was the only person beside Theresa who called Richard "Rick."

More guests began to trickle in soon afterward. Most of them were Richard's colleagues, or old family friends, and the children of those family friends, the ones Julie had been forced to pretend to like when she was younger. Now they greeted each other awkwardly, dancing around the fact that they had forgotten each other's names and shaking hands stiffly and muttering nondescript responses to questions about their lives. "Oh, you know how it is," and "Yep, I've been doing just fine," and "Pretty good, pretty good," were all favorites, although one curly-haired young man Julie vaguely remembered from his habit of picking his nose and his fascination with flora and fauna had just laughed when she asked him how things were going.

The living room and kitchen combined were only just large enough to hold all the people who'd come, and Julie soon found herself quite literally backed into a corner. She started trying to nudge her way through the crowd, passing very near Uncle Tommy, who had shown up at the party raving about the biography he'd read the week before on Nimitz. Julie didn't usually mind military history, but today was not the time, and this was not the place, for an extensive lecture. Especially not one delivered in Uncle Tommy's slow monotone.

Thankfully, however, she got to the food table without having been assaulted by "fun facts" about the Pacific Theater, and was able to load up on chicken wings and mashed sweet potatoes, which she piled high onto the flimsy paper plate.

The last time she'd seen her living room this crowded had been her brother's high school graduation party. There were people everywhere, sitting on the beat-up leather sofa and perched on the arms of the green velvet armchair or the mismatch of different folding chairs Julie had lugged up one by one from the basement. One person was even sitting on the sturdy wooden coffee table, which was about twice as old as Julie was and had, according to family legend, survived a crash in a moving van when it had been shipped from her grandparents' house in Iowa to Closefield Springs. Mostly, though, people stood around talking in clumps, weaving slightly, but not dancing, to the music still playing softly over the speakers. The buzz of dozens of different conversations wafted up to join in, making its own sort of music. Julie had always enjoyed watching people, and now she was happy to sit back and observe (aka eavesdrop on) the different interactions going on around her. She stood in the corner, eating her chicken and sweet potatoes, and watching a short bald man Julie was fairly certain was actually her godfather nod along as Rosie explained the various merits of adopting pets.

To their right, Richard was laughing at a story of a disastrous kayaking trip one of his old college friends was telling (with sound effects and even some acting). The trip ended when the kayaks were swept down the river with all the gear, at which point the man waved his arms about so violently that he accidentally hit Julie's godfather in the nose.

Julie tries to pass off a snort of laughter as a sudden coughing fit and turned to watch Annie and Trip chatting with the nose-picking botanist and a tall young woman who was known in childhood for having an extensive Barbie doll collection. Out of the corner of her eye, she saw Rosie fetching a wad of tissues for the godfather's nose, which had started to gush blood.

Then something clicked in Julie's mind, like a puzzle piece falling into place. It didn't make the whole picture clear, but suddenly hundreds of little things started to make sense. Well, more sense. Her chicken and sweet potatoes, which had been heavenly a moment before, seemed to turn to ash and sawdust in her mouth, and she dropped her plate into the nearest trash can and started shoving her way through the crowd.

"Sorry, pardon me, excuse me," she heard herself saying, as she barged through conversation circles, until she burst through the crowd into the deserted entryway. It was dark and empty and Julie spent a few moments leaning against the wall, taking deep breaths and trying to calm down and think clearly. It didn't help. Her mind was speeding like a race horse bursting through the gate. Thoughts flew through her head so quickly they hardly made sense. The staircase up to the second floor was on her right. The lights were off, and the staircase looked spooky and vaguely malicious in the strange shadows cast by the lights of the party. That would have bothered Julie, normally, but now her mind was filled with a single idea. She ran up the stairs, ancient muscle memory saving her from a misstep and a bad fall, because she certainly wasn't looking where she was going. She ran into her old bedroom and slammed the door shut behind her.

The room was exactly as she had left it. Her old bed was still there, covered in her old galaxy bedspread. Even the glow-in-the-dark stars stuck on the ceiling still shone faintly, well, some of them. Julie turned on the light, sat down on her bed, and pulled out her phone. It took her three tries to unlock it because her hands were shaking too badly to type. Finally, she got the phone open, and went to the email Luke had sent her. There were dozens of photos and videos, and she had to scroll through for what felt like ages before she found the one she was looking for. Four young boys standing in front of a rose bed in full bloom.

The roses were extraordinary specimens, that much was clear even viewed through an old photo by someone with the opposite of a green thumb. They were full and vibrant, petals ranging in color from dark orange to blood red.

"Oh my God," Julie whispered. Then she texted Trip: "My old room. Get up here NOW."

Five minutes passed, which Julie spend anxiously pacing the length of her room. Finally, she heard Trip's footsteps climbing up the stairs. Julie pulled him into the room and slammed the door shut.

"What's wrong?" Trip asked, looking worried.

"I need you to look at some song lyrics for me," Julie said, pulling up Caleb's song and handing her phone to Trip.

"What's this?"

"It's for the case," Julie said.

"'By Caleb Fredrick,' I knew it! You are looking into his murder!"

"Please, Trip, I think I'm close," Julie said.

"No," Trip said, shoving her phone back into her hands and starting for the door. "No way. You may be bent on this weird plan for self-destruction, but I'm certainly not going to help you."

Julie leaped in front of the door and blocked it. He tried to shove her aside, and she almost punched him, right then and there, but she held herself back just in time. She needed Trip, to confirm what she thought, what she suspected, the center, the eye, of the half-formed idea whirling like a bad storm in her mind.

"Please, Trip, I think I know who the killer might be, but I need your musician-y instincts to confirm it. If you won't, though, I'll just find another way, you know I will."

Trip chewed his lip for a full thirty seconds before answering, a thirty seconds Julie spent anxiously fidgeting as she waited for a response.

"Okay. I'll help you. But this is it."

Julie handed him the phone. He examined it for a while.

"What's it sound like?"

Julie played the recording. The song was sort of jazzy, sort of R&B, and sort of something Julie had never heard before, all at the same time.

"Huh," Trip said. "Never heard anything like it."

"Yeah, I know, but what does it mean?" Julie asked.

"Well, it's definitely giving off major 'defining moment' vibes, like those books they always made us read in high school,"

"A bildungsroman?"

"Whatever. But there're also overtones of some sort of violence, and I don't really understand the bit about a river, that could refer to a lot of different things. And I really don't understand the bit about the roses."

"Neither did I, at first, except that it seemed like a location. We thought it might be about rape, and maybe the rosebush was where it happened, except then it'd be 'in the roses' or 'behind the roses.' This says 'under the roses.'"

Trip's face went grayish pale, and he looked like he might be sick. "But what do you think now?"

Julie explained her theory, and watched as Trip's eyes went wide.

"So? Would that fit?"

"Yeah, it would, especially if it had anything to do with a river, how it happened, I mean, but… Jules, that's…"

"I know," Julie said. "Thank you, Trip. I've got to make some calls now. You should go on back to the party."

Trip nodded and left. Once the door was closed behind him, Julie locked it and made two calls. The first, to Clarissa Byron, gave her all the confirmation she needed. Then she called Ben.

While Julie had been greeting the first of the party guests, Ben had been driving to the radio station to see Brittany Burban. Every nerve in his body felt alight with tension. He tapped the steering wheel aggressively as he waited for the light to turn green, and had to restrain himself from laying on the horn when the car in front of him didn't immediately jump forward.

He parked in the shared lot between Roscoe's and the radio station and hopped out of the car, ignoring the fact that it was slightly crooked between the lines. He wanted to sprint, but he held himself back. Only an hour without Julie, and suddenly he was becoming the overeager one. Maybe ordinarily that thought would have made him smile, but he was too on edge for that now.

He threw open the double glass doors into the lounge in what he hoped was a dramatic manner, and walked over to the reception desk.

"Brittany Burban. Where is she?" he asked, but just then, he saw Brittany poking her platinum head out of the door to her office.

"What're you doing here?" she asked, glaring at him.

"Looking for you," Ben said. "Is there somewhere we can talk?"

Brittany looked like she might turn him away, but instead she pursed her lips until they turned white and let him into her office. It was a small, stuffy, and extraordinarily clean room with minimal furnishings, just the desk and two chairs.

"We have a witness who saw you arguing with Caleb Fredrick, just weeks before he died," Ben said, keeping his voice low.

Brittany didn't look evenly mildly frightened, as Ben had expected. "Where?" she demanded.

"At the Woodsley."

"But I didn't! I spent the first part of the night with Duke, and then I went for a swim at the pool, and then I went to bed, my own bed, that is."

"The witness saw you running down the stairs."

"Running? I don't remember… Oh! I was seen, when I was coming out of Duke's room, and I panicked."

Ben paused and thought for a moment.

"Was Duke's room near Caleb's?"

"Yes, across the hall, but I didn't hear any argument. We had music on."

"Was it Caleb, who saw you?"

"No."

"Was it someone coming out of his room?"

"Yes, I guess so."

"Who was it?"

Brittany told him.

His phone rang as he was getting back into his car.

"Yes?" he said.

Julie's voice was breathless. "I think I know who the killer is," Julie said.

"Me too. Let's see if our answers match," Ben said.

"It's just, well, all I have is a kind of guess, and it is backed up, a little, but not much. I can feel it, in my gut, though. Ah… It's hard to explain over the phone, it sounds crazy if I just say it out loud, I have to show you. Can we meet up after the party?"

Ben sighed. "We're having dinner with Lila's parents in a few hours," he said reluctantly. "And I've missed the last two, so I was ordered to attend this one."

"Oh," Julie said, and Ben knew she was just as reluctant to leave this until tomorrow as he was.

Ben made up his mind. "I can come over now," he said, hoping he sounded more confident than he felt. "You're at your parents' house, right?"

"Yeah, but, well, are you sure? I mean, my dad is here right now, it's his party, you do know that, right."

"I know," Ben said, his heart thumping loudly in his chest, "but I'll see you in half an hour."

CHAPTER 15:
Echoes of the Past

The party felt surreal to Julie now, like a fever dream, or a parallel world. She'd missed the blowing out of the candles, but someone, she thought it was her mother, put a plate with a slice of carrot cake into her hand, and she ate it robotically, not really tasting it, though normally it was one of her favorite desserts. People around her were talking, some of them talking to her, and she had to do her best to nod along, though to her they sounded like the adults in Charlie Brown. Faces blurred out in her mind, until she had no idea who she was currently pretending to listen to.

And then, finally, after what felt like eons, the sound of the doorbell cut through the fog of her mind. She rushed to the hall to greet Ben, but she was too late. Standing at the door, face to face with Ben for the first time in ten years, was Richard Bernard.

"What are you doing here?" Julie's father hissed, his hazel eyes narrowed. Julie came up and stood next to him.

"He's here for me, Dad. Let him in," Julie said, trying to stay calm, but her heartbeat was so loud she felt he would be able to hear it, hear her fear, like some sort of prowling predator.

"He's not setting foot in my house," Richard said, in that same, low, angry tone of voice.

"He's my boss, and you will let him in, because we've a murder to solve, and you of all people should know what that means."

"He's your... Your..." Richard stammered. "JULIE, WHAT IN GOD'S NAME WERE YOU THINKING?!"

The sounds of the party vanished from the background. Out of the corner of her eye, Julie saw a handful of guests poking their heads into the doorway to see what all of the commotion was about. Julie ignored them and stayed focused on her father, meeting his gaze dead on. There seemed to be a fire, burning behind his hazel eyes, but Julie didn't flinch.

"I wanted a job, he offered me one," Julie said calmly, and suddenly she realized that the calmness wasn't entirely fake, and his anger was only steeling her resolve, like hammer blows in the heat of a forge.

"Yeah, well, you're fired," Richard said.

"Not your call," Julie and Ben said at the same time. Richard looked stunned for a second. Then he slammed the door in Ben's face. Julie made to open it again, but her father blocked her and locked the door.

"This conversation is over," he said quietly.

"No, it's not," Julie said. "Can't you get it through your thick skull already? This is what I want to do, it's what I have to do, it's not just a job, it's a purpose. I think you know that, deep down."

"Find a different purpose."

"That's not how it works, and you know it. How would you feel, if Mom or your parents or Uncle Tommy told you to stop doing what you do?"

That gave Richard pause. Julie pressed her momentary advantage. "Let me see this through. You've always said I don't see things through, that I give up on things too easily. Let me prove you wrong."

Richard sighed. "Fine. You can go now, on one condition."

"Anything."

"I want your word that, after this is over, you'll quit your little job and find a safer one. One that won't put you in harm's way."

Julie bit her lip.

"Your call," Richard said. "Take it or leave it."

Julie closed her eyes. She counted to ten under her breath. She tried to think calmly, tried to think what the rational decision would be, tried to think if there was a way out of this without anyone getting hurt, but she was drawing a blank.

"You can't tell me what to do," Julie said, surprised by how cold her voice sounded. "It's my life. I'm not a child anymore. I can do whatever the fuck I want."

And with that, Julie shoved her father to the side, opened the door, and ran down the street after Ben.

She caught up to him halfway down the block, just before he climbed into his car.

"I'm here," she said.

"How'd you convince him to let you come?"

"We had a breakthrough," Julie said with a shrug, as she climbed into the passenger seat.

"I have the 'why,' and if I have the right 'who' then I have the 'how.'" Julie said, as they drove off.

"I have the 'who' for certain," Ben said. "Brittany Burban was the one Alex saw running down the stairs, but Alex only assumed that it was the same person who'd been arguing with Caleb, and that was where we got turned around. But Brittany did see the person who was. I just don't know why."

Julie explained her potential 'why,' and how she'd thought of it. "Don't you see? It all fits! The roses, even the reference to Trinity, it's got a triple meaning! I mean, there's the religious reference, of course, but also their little trinity, the three of them, and that getting broken. And the street, Trinity Lane, it went from a safe haven to a painful reminder."

"It's one heck of a leap," Ben said. "But I think you're right. Too many little things start to add up."

"And Caleb was going to reveal it to everyone! Which is why he was killed, the secret couldn't get out!"

"Right."

"Good. I'm glad you don't think I'm crazy. So what do we do now?"

"I think our best course of action is to call Arnold McMillan. He's in charge of the case, after all."

"Do you have his number?"

"Somewhere," Ben said, pointing to the glove compartment. "I wrote it down when all this started."

Julie opened the glove compartment and shone the light from her phone flashlight into it, shifting aside important papers, crumpled receipts, and a roadmap of Nebraska until she found a dingy blue post-it note with the initials A.M. and a phone number. She handed it to Ben, and he dialed it.

"Hello?" Ben said. There was a pause.

"It's Ben Clydesdale, remember, I called you weeks ago about the Caleb Fredrick case?"

There was another pause. Something said on the other end caused Ben to flinch slightly.

"It's not that I question your abilities," he said, before he seemed to be cut off.

"I believe I know who the killer is," Ben said quickly.

There was a very long pause.

"No, it wasn't a robbery."

"I'd prefer to come and explain it."

"Not possible? Do you hear what I'm saying, man? I've solved your case for you!"

"Yes, I'm bloody capable of solving a murder, I was a pol—"

"We think it's—"

Julie started checking her texts while Ben tried, sentence by interrupted sentence, to explain their theory. Suddenly, she saw a text from Luke that made her eyes go wide. She started waving at Ben, who held up a finger to silence her.

"Look, if I could just—"

But then he sighed and set down the phone. "He hung up on me."

Julie waved the phone at him. "Look!"

"I can't see anything, you're not holding it steady."

Julie tried to hold the phone still, but her hands were shaking too badly, so she gave up.. "Luke just texted. He's asking me if I know any music tech people who can help him with a show he's supposed to play this weekend, because guess who's leaving town?"

"Fuck!" Ben exclaimed, which made Julie giggle.

"Sorry," she said, when Ben glared at her. "I know this is serious, but I've just never heard you curse before."

Ben ignored that. "We don't have time to persuade McMillan."

"We gotta get to the apartment now," Julie said, but Ben was already pulling away from the curb and zooming down the street in what was probably just a bit over the speed limit.

There was no Beethoven that night. Instead, a tense silence filled the car. Julie's foot was bouncing up and down, up and down, and she couldn't stop it. Her hands trembled in her lap. Outside, the restaurants and businesses and offices that made up Closefield Springs flashed by. It was late enough that a lot of them were closed, their signs and windows dark and deserted-looking. Other signs were still brightly lit, other business were occupied or even crowded. They passed laughing teenagers as they emerged from a pizza place and a group of college-aged kids smoking something outside a bar.

Ben turned the corner into a residential area, and the light-up signs became lighted windows, winking out from the shadows. A family eating dinner. A couple watching TV.

And then they were in front of the apartment block.

"Is Clarissa going to be in?" Ben asked, as he parked the car in a spot marked "residents only."

Julie shivered as she opened the door and stepped out. "No. I called her during one of the commercial breaks, and she mentioned she'd be staying a bit later. She and Duke have each taken over half of Caleb's old slot, until Brittany and Lianna can find a replacement. She'll be out until 10:00."

"Good."

They walked up to the building. Julie took a deep breath to steady her nerves, and double-checked the apartment number she'd gotten from Clarissa, which she'd written down on a scrap of notebook paper. The elevator was broken, and they had to take the stairs. The stairwell was dark and deserted and Julie was glad when they reached the sixth floor and a lit hallway. Ben knocked on the door marked 603, but there was no response.

"Try the roof," Julie suggested. "He likes being up over the city, he told me so."

They went back into the creepy stairwell and climbed a floor up, but then the stairs stopped. Julie looked around and wondered if there was even any way to get up onto the roof, but then Ben spied a narrow ladder leading to a blue-painted hatch in the ceiling marked "roof access." Julie climbed up first and tested the hatch. To her surprise, it was unlocked. She pushed it open, climbed through, and waited for Ben to follow.

He poked his head up, hauled himself through, and slammed the hatch shut. Then he drew out a small flashlight from his pocket and turned it on, and to Julie's surprise, the bright beam illuminated not one young man up on the roof with them, but two. She recognized Luke's shaggy dark hair, glistening in the light from the flashlight, and she felt her stomach drop. She didn't want him to hear this. But she pressed on anyway.

"Hi, Cameron," she said, and Cameron Little turned to face her. She could see it in his eyes that he knew why they were there. "Are you going to tell Luke, or should we?"

"Tell me what?" Luke demanded.

Ben kept his voice level. No need to panic either of them with anger or aggression. "Cameron's known what happened to Danny all this time, Luke, and he's never told a single soul."

Luke turned to Cameron. His voice came out shaky and small and pleading. "Cam?"

"I'd sit down, if I were you," Julie advised, but Luke had already collapsed to the ground. He looked like he'd been struck down by a sledgehammer. Or rammed through with a train. Or both at once.

"Why don't you tell us about it?" Ben asked.

"I don't…" Cameron stammered out, and in the beam of white light, Julie could see true fear in his eyes. "I don't know what you're… What you're… What you're…"

"There've been enough lies already, Cam," Julie said. "Don't you think it's time to tell the truth?"

When Cameron spoke, his voice was choked. "It was an accident," he said. "We were playing, up on the hill, near the creek. We were sword-fighting, with some sticks we'd found, it was Danny's idea. I didn't want to, but he kept pressing us, called us chickens. He didn't like cowards, Danny, he always said. He always said that. It always made me so mad. So I was angry at him, I was hitting harder, harder than I should have, and then I got him good, a real solid blow to his chest, hard enough to break my stick, and he was knocked backwards." Cameron swallowed and continued, and suddenly Julie flashed back to her lunch with Luke. Cameron describing his incident was so very similar to the way she'd described hers. "We were up, on a sort of hill, kind of a small cliff, really, and when Danny fell back, he lost his footing and fell, and tumbled down into the stream. Cal and I went to go check on him, but we took the slower way, we went around, there's a little deer track that's not quite as steep, easier to use, and we thought he'd be fine, the water was shallow, but I guess he hit his head on the way down, and we took too long, and by the time we got there, he'd drowned."

With every word Cameron spoke, a little more of Luke's soul seemed to leave him. Cameron was too caught up in his own story to notice. "We didn't know what to do, and we panicked. In the end, we waited until nightfall, and then we snuck back and buried Danny in the backyard. The Sebastians' fence was really low, it was the only one we could hop over carrying him."

"Under the rosebush, right?" Julie prompted. Cameron nodded.

"We wanted to have something to remember him, like a grave marker, sort of. The roses are pretty, and Danny always liked them, we thought he'd be happy, we thought he'd like it there."

"And then what?" Ben asked.

"We went back to our campsite, and got rid of the rest of Danny's things. Dumped them in the creek, where they got washed out to who knows where. Probably at the bottom of the Chesapeake by now."

"And you told everyone you'd thought he'd run away. But Danny Sebastian never left Trinity Lane, he's still there."

Cameron nodded.

"But Caleb never really liked keeping it all a secret, did he?" Julie asked. "All these years, it was eating away at him, that he knew what happened to Danny, that he could give his family some peace and closure, but he couldn't reveal anything without implicating himself. One day, about three years ago, he finally made up his mind. He started working on a song, a tribute to Danny, and he was going to confess after it was released," Julie said.

"He told me at the Woodsley, that this was his plan. He showed me the song, even. But it wasn't just his secret to keep, I would lose everything I'd ever worked for. He wouldn't listen to me, so I stormed out."

"And you ran into Brittany Burban, coming out of Duke Werkle' room," Ben said.

"That was who that was? She ran away, before I could get a good look at her."

"Yep."

Cameron shook his head to refocus, and began again. "But then Caleb didn't mention our argument, or coming forward, or even the song for the rest of the trip, so I thought the matter was dropped."

"Until a couple weeks later, when Caleb called you and told you to meet him and Luke for lunch," Julie said.

Cameron turned to Luke, now. "I couldn't let him tell you," he said, and in the beam of Ben's flashlight, Julie could see that both men were crying, their tears reflective silver in the light. "Even if he just played the song, even if he hadn't said a word, you would have understood. I had to do something."

"And you figured you would have a chance at Clarissa's party," Julie said. "It was right next to the radio station, and you were able to slip out long enough to go and talk to Caleb."

Cameron was close to full on sobbing by now. "I thought maybe I could get him to see reason, but he didn't budge, he stayed firm. But I just couldn't let him tell anyone. Then he turned his back to walk away, and suddenly I'd grabbed a knife and I just… I just… I didn't realize I'd done it until he fell to the floor. I wiped the knife handle clean, and grabbed Caleb's wallet, since I was pretty sure that was where he kept the flash drive. I dragged Caleb behind the sofa. Figured it would buy me some time, maybe. I dunno what I was thinking, I guess I wasn't, really. I felt all numb inside. And then I went back to the party. I told

Clarissa that I felt sick, that I'd been throwing up in the bathrooms, and that bit was true, I did puke afterwards. I went home, crawled into bed, hoped it would all go away, but the nightmare didn't end, and when I woke up, I figured the cops would be knocking on the door any minute. I didn't ever expect to get away with it, but I guess they assumed robbery… And then you guys came around, and you were looking into it, and you asked about Danny, but I couldn't tell you the truth, because it was all worse now, all a million times worse. So I decided to leave."

Cameron finished speaking. No one said anything for a full minute. Then Luke leaped to his feet. "How could you?" he cried, and he would have charged Cameron, but Ben leapt for him and held him back. Luke struggled for a moment in the larger man's arms, but then went limp as an overcooked noodle. "I trusted you," he said, his pained voice hardly more than a whisper. "I can't believe I trusted you."

"I know you did," Cameron said with a wince.

"Well, it's time to go back," Ben said. Cameron shook his head.

"I can't, don't you see?" Cameron said, and he looked up. Julie recognized the look in his eyes, though she'd seen it only once before, a long time ago, in the eyes of a small-time drug dealer just moments before he'd put a bullet in her stomach. "There's no way out."

"There's always a way out," Julie said, and for the second time that day, she realized that, though every logical thought in her head was screaming that she ought to be scared, terrified, even, she felt totally calm. Maybe it was courage. Maybe it was recklessness. Maybe it was nothing more noble than complete and utter stupidity, but she didn't feel afraid at all. Her mind felt clearer than it had in years.

Cameron, however, was less serene. He took a few halting steps backward, toward the ledge. "Not for me," he said. "There's no way out for me."

"Please, come back with us," Julie begged, taking a small step forward. In the beam of Ben's flashlight, she could see Cameron's shoulders shaking. The icy winds tossed his blond curls about. She took another step forward, and then another. She was close enough to reach out and touch him now. She took his trembling, sweaty hand in her own. "Let's go, Cam. I'm sorry."

"Not as sorry as I am," Cameron whispered, and he tried to shove her away as he leaped over the side, but the rooftop was slick with ice, and Julie slipped to the side and suddenly there was nothing beneath her but icy air, and she was plummeting down toward the alley below, down… She flailed wildly as she fell, scrabbling at the bricks for a handhold, trying to find something, anything, that would slow her fall. One hand connected with a windowsill, and she jerked to a halt, her shoulder nearly popping out of its socket, but she managed to get her other hand up and hold on for dear life, finding a strength deep down that she didn't know she had. Beneath her, she saw Cameron, his eyes closed, his arms outstretched, as he plummeted. For the briefest of moments, he looked almost peaceful. Then he slammed into the cold hard pavement with a sickening crack.

Julie's fingers were screaming, but she hung on, because letting go meant death, she was still so high up… With a flash of blinding panic, she felt herself slipping, and she tried to tighten her grip, but it seemed to make little difference.

She could hear Ben and Luke, far above her, calling out their names.

"I'm here!" she yelled back, but she knew she was too far down to be easily rescued. A gust of icy wind nearly blew her away from the wall.

Her fingers started to bleed where the brick cut into them, her blood turning the stone dark and making it slick as wet soap. She was still slipping, bit by bit, millimeter by millimeter. Then another gust of wind blew through, and suddenly her fingers had closed on nothing but air, and the ground was rushing up to meet her.

Julie crashed into the open dumpster. The cushioning of so many leaking plastic bags saved her life.

CHAPTER 16:
Parting Ways

Ben was about to walk through the open door when he heard hushed voices inside. He peeked through the opening carefully, and decided he didn't want to disturb the meeting. A tall redhead he didn't recognize was sitting in one of the uncomfortable plastic chairs next to Julie's bed. There were tears in both girls' eyes, but their voices, while serious, were not urgent, and they were smiling, so Ben figured it was something important, but not necessarily bad. They hugged, and the redhead left, passing Ben on her way out.

Ben poked his head into the room.

"Hey," he said, sitting down in the chair the redhead had vacated. "Who was that?"

"Katie, she came by to apologize, but I apologized first. I shouldn't have gotten so worked up, and she was only ever trying to keep me safe. We're cool now. I'm glad, I don't like it when we're not talking," Julie said, as she wiped the tears from her eyes with her bandaged hands.

"How do you feel?"

"Oh, never better," Julie said with a shadow of her impish grin. "You?"

"I'm fine, but as you recall, it wasn't me who fell off a building, now was it?"

"All part of my genius plan," Julie said.

"They found a shoebox under Cameron's bed. It had Caleb's wallet in it, including the original flash drive."

"And Danny?"

"Under the old rosebushes. Like Cameron said. You were right."

"I'm always right."

"Yeah, well, don't go getting a big head over it," Ben said, and for a second, he smiled, but then his brown eyes turned somber. "What's next then? For you?"

"Not sure. I'll figure it out."

"Maybe you can be a mystery writer next," Ben suggested, trying and failing to sound upbeat. He tried to imagine his office without Julie lounging in the armchair, or blowing massive grape-flavored bubbles, or generally annoying the heck out of him, and he had to fight a lump forming in his throat.

"Yeah," Julie said, and Ben wondered if she was thinking the same things. "That could be..." She trailed off. She'd meant to say 'fun' but the word had refused to materialize.

"Well," Ben said, checking his watch. "I'd better get going. Lila's been quite strict about curfew lately. Can't imagine why."

Julie tried to laugh. It hurt. "Good. Save the getting hurt for me, okay? I don't want you muscling in on my territory."

"Yeah," Ben said, trying his best to smile. "Take care, Jules."

He stood to leave just as Richard Bernard came in through the door, carrying a Coca-Cola can in one hand and a pack of grape-flavored gum in the other.

The two men stared at each other for a moment, while Julie squirmed awkwardly behind them.

Finally, Ben broke the silence. "I'm sorry, I was just leaving," he said.

Richard nodded curtly. Ben stepped past him out into the hallway.

Lila was waiting for him in the parking garage.

"How is she?" she asked, as Ben slid into the passenger's seat.

"She'll be okay, I think," Ben said.

"And you?"

"Yeah. I'm fine."

It was late in the little town of Closefield Springs, as Lila pulled into the driveway, but a good few people were still awake. Ben and Lila got out of their car and walked up the front steps, together, hand in hand. The doorknob stuck a bit, like it always did, before swinging open to let the couple into their home, where they settled down to watch The Chronicles of Myst: Episode 5: The Dark Apprentice and eat cheap Italian food.

In her dark living room, Clarissa Byron was lying curled up in a ball on the couch, not really paying attention to what was playing on the television. On the coffee table in front of her was a polaroid photograph of a curly-haired, dark-eyed young man, his head thrown back in laughter. She glanced over at the photograph and had to swallow back tears.

A few miles north, Luke Sebastian sat on the back patio of his childhood home. He was only wearing a light jacket, but he didn't seem to feel the cold. He took another swig from his flask, which glinted in the moonlight, and stared out with glazed eyes at the mound of upturned earth in the back corner of the yard.

Downtown, sitting in her parents' recording studio, Alex Harcourt posted Caleb Fredrick's final work on YouTube. She had thought long and hard about what to name the song. Caleb had never included a name in his notes. Alex had asked a few times if he had any ideas, for a title, but he had just shrugged, said he'd know the perfect one when it came to him. Alex hoped that Caleb would approve of the name she had chosen. "Danny's Roses."

EPILOGUE:

It was more than just a brief respite from winter's cold, but the first real, proper, bright spring day of the year. Ben sat alone in the corner of the familiar room, watching a basketball game on the battered television set that hung precariously over the bar and trying to ignore the squeaks the barstool made every time he moved an inch.. Late afternoon sun drifted in through the green stained-glass windows, illuminating the dust particles that hung in the air. Music played softly in the background on the grimy speakers in the corner.

The door opened and a young woman came in. Ben almost didn't recognize her. Her hair had been cut short, so that it bobbed around her ears as she moved, and her clothes were clean, not rumpled or stained. Her hazel eyes, though, the way they glinted in that clever and mischievous way he'd come to love, were unmistakable.

"Hi," Julie said, as she took the seat next to Ben's. "I was hoping I'd find you here."

"You look… better," Ben said, and it was the truth. She seemed brighter, somehow. There were no shadows under her eyes, and her shoulders didn't seem as weighed down. It was as if clouds had parted, and the sun was finally shining through again. This was Julie as he'd always hoped she'd be, more whole, more… complete.

"I feel good," Julie said, tucking a lock of hair behind her ears.

"Even though it happened again? Getting hurt, I mean?"

Julie shrugged. "It's like… Before it felt like I was waiting, waiting for my life to begin properly. But now, that part of me has been filled, I guess. Or maybe it's like a double negative. This time almost dying canceled out last time almost dying."

Ben raised an eyebrow. "I don't think it works like that."

Julie grinned and then looked thoughtful for a moment. "I think…" she said slowly. "I think what makes this time different is that I know now I can't run away from it, all those feelings."

"What does that mean for you going forward?" Ben asked.

Julie looked down at her hands. Her fingers were criss-crossed with faint white scars. "I… Well, that's part of why I'm here, actually. Last night, I went over and talked to my dad. Really talked, and really listened too for once. We had a really good conversation, actually, and in the end, we agreed that my choices regarding my future, my profession, are mine to make."

Julie raised her head a little, peeking out at Ben from underneath her caramel-colored locks.

Ben grinned. "You know, I happen to have an opening. If you're interested."

Julie sat up straight. She could feel her heartbeat like hammer blows in her chest, like a steady drum beat in a good song.

"What do you say?" Ben asked. "Partners?"

Julie smiled, a full, bright smile, spring sunshine melting away the frost. "Yeah. Partners."